ONE NIGHT AT THE SKULL SPARK CLUB

DRAYTON FALLS VOLUME 3

BRYAN SMITH

Grindhouse Press #115
ISBN-13: 978-1-957504-28-5

This one is for all the rock and roll kids of the 70s and 80s. All the other creaky old headbangers and punk rockers who keep the spirit of that era's music alive in their hearts to this day. Decades (and decades) may pass, and bodies may falter and weaken, memories might fade and become blurry, but a trip back to the past is always just a twist of the volume knob away.

TABLE OF CONTENTS

ONE NIGHT AT THE SKULL SPARK CLUB

ONE MINUTE CRAIG KING HAD his eyes fixed on the dark road ahead, feeling good from the three strong craft beers circulating in his system and the rock and roll music playing loud enough to make the windows of his Corolla vibrate, and then at some indistinct point, he slipped into blackness.

The next thing he knew, strong hands were slapping at him and loud, shrill voices were screaming. It took him a split second to realize the voices weren't the recorded vocals on some old heavy metal song, that they were instead the voices of his old friends raised in terrified alarm. The world was bleary, out-of-focus, and a little smear of light floating in the semi-darkness just below eye level. The screaming intensified as he squeezed his eyes shut and immediately opened them wide again, by which point his vision had cleared enough to grasp the source of concern.

His car had veered over the double yellow lines dividing the two-lane road and was now fully in what would be the correct lane if they were out for a drive in the English countryside. Unfortunately, they were *not* out for a ride in the English countryside but were instead traveling along a sparsely illuminated back road in Drayton Falls, which was in America, where this side of the road was emphatically the *wrong* side.

Craig sat up straighter in his seat. "Whoops. Shit."

He'd blacked out behind the wheel. Only for a few seconds, most likely, but this was a circumstance where a mere moment of inattention (or an unanticipated lapse into unconsciousness) could mean the difference between life and death. Further complicating matters was another belated realization, one that came hot on the heels of the first and was perhaps even more alarming.

The leftward drift of the Corolla was still in-progress. If he didn't take corrective action within about one more second, the front of the car would bounce over the shoulder and smash through the guardrail, beyond which was a rocky ravine of sufficient depth to render this a fatal event.

Craig and his passengers were saved from disaster at the last possible instant when the person riding in the shotgun seat seized hold of the steering wheel and wrenched it hard to the right. The Corolla veered away from the shoulder and back toward the double yellow lines, straddling the lines instead of returning fully to the proper lane.

Bright headlights loomed in the opposite direction, approaching fast, growing bigger and brighter by each fractional second. Staring impending doom in the face yet again, Craig at last snapped free of the trance of stunned amazement that had gripped him. He steered the Corolla fully into the correct lane seconds before a redneck's heavy-duty pickup truck went thundering by them, shuddering in terror at the near miss while cringing at the loud gasps of relief and shouted recriminations from his passengers.

He pulled over on the road's right-hand shoulder, put the car in park, squelched the volume on the music, and said, "You know what? I'm thinking maybe someone else should drive."

There came a moment of pregnant silence.

The aftermath was outrage tinged with terror at the close call.

Bill Hudson, riding shotgun, slugged him hard in the shoulder. "Motherfucker! What the hell happened?"

"Yeah, Jesus fuck," came the voice of the sole backseat passenger, Stacy Whittaker. She was breathing heavily, and a glance at the rearview showed she had a trembling hand pressed to her chest. "I thought you'd had a heart attack at the wheel or some shit. My life flashed before my fucking eyes. I mean, not literally, but you know what I mean."

A troublemaker in days long gone by, her voice carried a tinge of that old manic quality that once upon a time had signaled dire impending danger for the target of her ire. Of the three of them, she was the only one with an actual criminal record. Nothing serious on a felony level, but she'd spent some months behind bars for various scrapes she'd gotten in. All of that was so long ago it'd become easy to forget she'd once been capable of that level of volatility.

Also once upon a long-ass time ago, Stacy and Craig were an item, living together in a shithole apartment for several years. This was when they were in their late teens and early twenties. It seemed like something from another lifetime, like something that had happened to other people entirely, each of them bore so little resemblance to the people they'd been in those desperate, near-penniless days of scrounging change to buy six-packs of Schaefer beer or bottles of Mad Dog 20/20. Or other, less legal stuff.

Their eyes met for a moment in the mirror.

Stacy grunted and looked away.

Sometimes at night when he was in bed next to his wife of thirty-plus years, a woman whose own feelings for him had changed considerably, he'd think of those long-ago days in that horror show of an apartment with Stacy and try to remember how it'd felt to experience real passion. He could summon the memories, bring the blurred images into his brain, but connecting with the actual feelings he'd had when he was young had become so much harder. Sometimes, often, he thought that was what he hated most about getting old.

The loss of that fire.

Sometimes, every once in a while, out of nowhere he'd experience a faint, flickering reminder, and it'd make the ache of that loss that much worse.

The music from the radio was still just audible, despite having been turned down. Several seconds elapsed with no one saying a word, the only sound the faint strains of "Generation Nowhere" by the Bile Lords. It'd been the B-side to "Locked and Loaded", the first single from *Hollywood Babylon*, their first and most successful album.

Bill Hudson said, "Hard to believe we're about to see these guys again. In less than an hour. Been a long time."

Craig nodded. "Yeah."

Another conversational silence ensued. Craig shifted slightly in his seat, fighting his body's urge to squirm in discomfort. In bygone days, he'd loved the people with him tonight as much as any blood relative.

An echo of that feeling still existed, but it was a compartmentalized emotion, a carefully preserved relic of another time. A thing that got set aside and left almost forgotten for long periods. They'd text each other once in a blue moon, but in-person hangouts had become depressingly rare. Rare, but not nonexistent. Once every year or two, something would come about to bring them together again for a short time. Something compelling enough to cause them to shake off the dust of years and remember they were friends who used to spend virtually all their waking time together, along with some other people who were no longer around.

In this case, it was Bill Hudson who alerted them to the astonishing news that the Bile Lords were coming to Drayton Falls. Just over a week ago, Craig was mired in a miserably dull planning meeting at work when his phone buzzed, signaling the arrival of a text.

Sneaking a quick glance, all he saw in the text preview was the name of the person who'd messaged him and a single word bracketed by multiple exclamation marks: !!!DUDE!!!

Many months had elapsed since the last time he'd heard from Bill. Most of a year. But the excitement conveyed in that one word stirred his curiosity enough to hold his attention. Instead of setting the phone down after the usual perfunctory message check, he glanced up and saw that his boss was standing with his back turned to him at the far end of the conference table, pointing to something on a projection screen.

Something he should probably be paying attention to, actually, but instead he tapped the message preview to expand it and saw a photo Bill had taken of a black-and-white flyer stapled to a city utility pole. The flyer advertised an upcoming show by the Bile Lords at a place called the Skull Spark Club. Craig had never heard of the club, though later he would look it up and discover it'd once been the Silver & Gold Bar & Grill, a place where he and his old pals had seen local bands and low-level national acts many times in the golden olden days, but never anyone as noteworthy as the fucking Bile Lords.

Not even close.

It boggled the imagination.

After the meeting let out, Craig hurried back to his desk and texted his friend back in a similarly excited manner: *THE FUCK!? That can't be real!*

But it was real, all right, as some additional online investigation soon verified. The date was even listed on the band's official website as part of its itinerary on the so-called *Rituals of Babylon* tour, which had been launched a month prior in support of an upcoming new album by that name.

Later that day, Craig called Stacy to relay the news, and at first she was equally disbelieving. She was cooking her dinner and trying to rush him off the phone, but he urged her in his most adamant tone, one he later realized was reminiscent of his younger self, to go to the band's site and see for herself.

Sighing in exasperation, she kept him on the line as she did just that.

Then came a long pause.

And after that, another sigh, albeit one with a different tenor. "Well, shit. We're going, I guess?"

Of course they were. And they were almost there.

Bill nudged him in the shoulder again. "Hop out, man. I'll drive."

After switching places, they resumed their journey to the Skull Spark Club. The volume on the music went back up a bit again, but not enough to prohibit conversation.

Bill glanced at Craig as they idled at a red light. "Can't believe you passed out. Thought you only had three of those fancy beers at dinner. Or did you pregame before we met up?"

Stacy said, "Probably slammed a quart of Jack and chased it with some *co*-caine."

That was how she'd always said the word in the old days, with an extra emphasis on the first syllable. Craig had no idea how long it'd been since he'd last heard that particular verbal tic of hers. Decades, maybe.

He laughed. "Where would I have done that? At home? I don't think so. Janine would be serving me divorce papers the next fucking day. And, shit, if I'd done any coke, I sure the fuck wouldn't have been blacking out after just three motherfucking beers, high ABV or not."

Before anyone could reply to that, it hit him that Stacy wasn't the only one lapsing into speech patterns of old. These days he didn't go around enlivening his sentences with so many variations of the word fuck. It wasn't that he'd become a prude in his old age. He still said it at appropriate moments, but he didn't salt multiple uses of the word into his every utterance anymore. The habit had waned considerably after the birth of his daughter twenty-five years ago.

They all had kids.

Stacy had a girl and a boy, both grown. Bill had several kids from two marriages, the majority from the second, still-enduring union. Craig didn't even know all their names. His Hannah was an only child. He couldn't imagine the sheer gargantuan scope of everything that went into raising and being responsible for a brood the size of Bill's. It'd probably drive him insane.

Stacy made a noise of contempt. "The fuck is an ABV?"

Bill chuckled. "Alcohol by volume. What, you not up on your beer snob terminology, Stacy?"

She made another scoffing sound. "If it don't say Pabst Blue Ribbon or Miller fuckin' High Life on the label, I don't know shit about it."

Craig smirked. "Still a lady of refined tastes after all these years."

Bill and Craig glanced at each other, shared a subdued laugh.

A silent beat passed.

Then Stacy said, "Oh, I'd say I've gotten a *lot* more discerning over the years. Dumped your sorry ass, didn't I?"

Bill winced as he glanced again at his old buddy, now riding shotgun. "Ooh. Sick burn."

Bill and Stacy laughed.

Craig forced a smile. He wanted to laugh along with them, but in truth her words triggered an unexpected twist in his guts. It didn't feel quite like a full reopening of that old wound, but it pulled hard at the stitches. Not just the words themselves, but the tone in which they were uttered. Lighthearted in a discernibly fake way, with an undercurrent of bitterness and spite. Craig knew Stacy didn't hate him, but he also knew she carried a weight of submerged hurt that never entirely went away. Yeah, she "dumped" him, but it was only because he drove her to it by betraying her.

But calling what he'd done a "betrayal" was the nice way of putting it. "Betrayal" was such a quaintly ordinary word, one better applied to trust transgressions of a more standard type. Not so much for fucking the half-sister of your girlfriend less than a week after hinting you might want to marry her.

Sensing his unease, Bill gave the old Corolla's volume knob a twist, turning the music up louder for the crashing opening chords of "Nasty Thing", the penultimate track on side two of *Hollywood Babylon*. Hard-driving and laced with profanity, it was not a radio-friendly track at all, but it'd always been one of their favorites.

Bill and Stacy raised their voices to sing along, and after a few moments, the tension began to lessen. Craig smiled and sang along with his friends. It was stupid to let that ancient history spoil the fun.

They were all too old for that shit.

More than thirty years ago. Christ. It was another fucking life. Let it go.

Craig's mood lifted even more after they took a right turn and the lights of the Skull Spark Club came into view. The brick building was painted black now, but it was still recognizably the same place, down to the falling-down old fence of leaning wooden posts held together by a few strands of rusted barbed wire that ringed most of the smallish parking lot in front.

By the time they pulled into the lot, it was less than forty minutes until showtime. The joint wasn't exactly hopping, with only a scattering of other vehicles present. They could have parked right outside the entrance, but Bill opted to back the Corolla into a corner spot at the rear of the lot. As he cut the engine, a faint sound of muffled music could be heard from the club. It sounded like a live performance rather than recorded music.

Stacy scooted forward, poking her head through the gap between the front seats, her frowning gaze directed toward the black-painted building. "That's just the opening band, right? We're not late for the Lords."

Craig twisted in his seat to look at her, nodding as he said, "No, that's the opening band. Some local kids. Wings of Smoke, they call themselves. I called to confirm earlier. They would've went on about twenty minutes ago, based on what I was told."

"So we've got a little time."

Craig shrugged. "A little."

Stacy leaned back again and a moment later they heard her rooting around in her purse. Seconds later came the spark of a lighter, followed shortly by a familiar aromatic odor. Then she popped into the gap between seats again, nudging Craig before pushing a cheap plastic Bic and a small glass weed pipe into his hands.

Craig brought the pipe to his mouth and flicked the lighter. He did this with a twinge of trepidation, a little dread about what could happen if they got a tad carried away with the intoxicants tonight. At their age, none of them were built for hardcore partying. It wouldn't be right to go to a rock and roll show and not have a little taste of this and that, but a taste was all it should be. He could too easily imagine the look of scorn Janine would give him if he came home reeking of weed and high-octane booze. But this was the old ride or die crew.

They'd gone to so many shows together and this was part of their ancient ritual, the pre-show buzz boost. He told himself it'd be okay as long as he kept it to a quick toke or two, then he'd mellow out by nursing one or two weak-ass beers the rest of the night. PBR or some other shit like that. Stacy beers.

Craig took a deep inhale.

Then he fired up the pipe and took a bigger one.

Bill snatched the lighter and pipe from his hands and did the same. Stacy then reclaimed her paraphernalia and hit it yet again. When Craig and Bill each waved off another go, they got out of the car and went into the club.

The interior had a "the same but different" look and feel. On the surface, nothing drastic had changed since the Silver & Gold days. A dark foyer lined with narrow leather-upholstered couches was exactly as Craig remembered, down to the cracks in the upholstery and the Guns N' Roses pinball game still tucked away in a corner. Through a vaulted arch and then around a corner to the left was the bar. Inside, the lighting was dim and yellow-tinted. The barstools looked as if they might be the same ones he'd sat on when he'd been a semi-regular here decades ago. More waves of head-spinning nostalgia assailed him virtually everywhere he looked.

A wooden rail still separated the small bar area from the marginally larger space reserved for dining, where a handful of rickety round tables were ringed by plastic-backed chairs with chrome legs. The curved seats of the chairs triggered new tingles of anticipatory dread. Chairs of that time were fine when he was in his twenties, but Craig had a hunch they might play hell on his back now. The only other options were to stand in the open area in front of the little stage or sit at the bar, the latter being a problem as there were not enough open stools for all three of them.

Despite the enduring presence of so much of the old decor, the vibe felt subtly different, darker in ways both literal and figurative. The walls inside were all painted black to match the brick exterior. In the olden days, the walls were a bright, almost festive shade of neon red. The change of shade matched the subdued mood of the sparse crowd. Even the handful of people standing in front of the stage struck Craig as dour for a rock and roll crowd. The band was pounding out some slow and heavy if somewhat generic sludge/doom riffage in a competent way, but there wasn't much in the way of headbanging going on.

In fact, no headbanging at all was occurring.

It was strange.

Perhaps it was a passe form of expression. Craig didn't know. Too many years had passed since his last excursion to a sleaze pit rock club to have any clue. Or maybe these kids were too disaffected to show anything resembling enthusiasm for the performance they were watching. One young woman had her phone out and was recording the band as they played, which Craig knew was a common thing at shows these days. Curiously, she was the only doing that. The rest of the dozen or so other spectators were either standing stock-still or swaying almost imperceptibly. One young woman scuffed her shoes at the concrete floor in a way he first took as an awkward form of dancing, but he soon realized she was either stoned to the brink of total insensibility or blind drunk. She wasn't "dancing", she was trying not to pass out and collapse to the floor. From the look of things, it was a battle she was unlikely to win. Craig hoped she wasn't here alone. She looked like she wasn't even legal drinking age. He wondered if her parents had any idea where she was or what she was doing tonight.

The whole tableau was just *weird*.

Looking around, he'd never felt so old in his life. The drunk girl and the rest of them weren't doing anything he hadn't done a million times when he was their age. All but one among the small group standing in front of the stage looked roughly the same age as drunk girl, or no more than a few years older. The lone exception was a scrawny man in a loose-fitting black t-shirt whose sun-weathered arms and heavily lined face gave him away as being even older than Craig and his friends. A vintage black Bile Lords ballcap sat atop the man's head, turned backward, as was briefly the Axl Rose-inspired fashion in the early 90s. At least a dozen other old heads—not counting Craig and his crew—sat either at the tables or occupied the majority of stools at the bar. The floor and seated areas felt segregated by age, by default if not by rule.

Except for that one skinny old rebel, more power to him.

Stacy leaned in close as they stood at the rail and half-watched the band, raising her voice to be heard above the music. "First round's on me, boys." She gave Craig a shove toward the end of the rail. "Go on, get us a table."

She turned away and moved toward the bar before Craig could object. Thinking of his intention to nurse one or two weak beers, he settled for shouting at her to get him a PBR. Her back was to him, but she raised a hand, flipping it vaguely in their direction, which he chose to take as confirmation of his request.

Then he looked at Bill, shrugging as he said, "I guess we're sitting at a table."

The pained look that passed his friend's face suggested Bill shared his comfort worries on that count, but what could they do?

Craig led the way and selected a table closest to the open area in front of the stage. Roughly a dozen feet of empty space stood between them and the loose gaggle of standing spectators. Chair legs scraped concrete as they were pulled away from the table, each man wincing as they settled tender old posteriors and creaky backs into the molded hard plastic.

Several minutes went by as they waited for Stacy to return with their drinks.

Becoming impatient, Craig turned his head to look toward the bar and saw she'd wedged herself between two stools and was leaning against the bar as she chatted with a leather-vested old biker in a gray ponytail. A man stationed behind the bar was pouring drinks, but he was grinning and obviously tuned into the conversation between Stacy and the biker. Craig couldn't read lips, but he could venture a guess at the subject matter. She was still a shameless flirt. Biker dude would probably end up paying for her drinks. The thought brought a smirk to his face, but the expression froze when he saw the biker put a meaty hand speckled with age spots on her hip. Just for a second, he felt a stirring of the jealous rage that always used to come over him when he saw guys getting handsy with his girl.

But Stacy wasn't his girl anymore.

Hadn't been since Bill Clinton's first term.

Still, the feeling lingered a beat or two longer than felt comfortable. He became a touch more acutely aware of how sexy Stacy could still be when she wanted. Sexy in a more age-worn way, true, but sexy nonetheless, especially at just the right distance and in dim lighting. Like the current conditions. Tonight the impression was enhanced by how she'd dressed herself up for a rock and roll show. Studded black leather jacket open over a tight New York Dolls shirt, tight jeans with several holes allowing for tantalizing glimpses of hidden tattoos, and black boots. A white Bile Lords skull and chains logo was painted on the back of the jacket. Worn by a younger person, Craig would suspect the jacket was a thrift store acquisition, but she'd had it as long as he'd known her. He still remembered the weekend she'd spread it out on the kitchen table in their old apartment to paint it, the band's latest CD at the time playing on repeat on the stereo, an ever-present scent of cheap dragon's blood incense in the air.

Craig looked away.

Across the table, Bill raised an eyebrow. "You okay?"

Craig feigned a look of confusion. "Yeah. Why wouldn't I be?"

Bill had no immediate reply, instead choosing to redirect his gaze to the stage, where a long song by Wings of Smoke was barreling its way to a drawn-out conclusion. The sound was heavy, but the kids in the band looked nearly as apathetic as the onlookers. After the song's final crashing chords rang out, a squall of feedback followed, a sound that also went on longer than seemed necessary.

When all was finally silent, a tall kid with long black hair hanging in his face like Joey Ramone stepped to the front of the stage, sighed forlornly into the microphone, waited an extra moment, and mumbled the band's parting words: "We have been Wings of Smoke. Have a pleasant evening."

Then they began the process of breaking down their equipment and removing it from the stage, going about it in a listless, unhurried manner. The slow-motion way they moved made it appear they were all under the influence of some heavy-duty sedative. Or heroin.

Once again, Bill and Craig locked gazes across the table.

Bill raised a hand to flash devil horns. "Metal, dude."

The way he said it, in a tone of the profoundest apathy, brought an unexpected burst of laughter from Craig. Then they were both laughing, their amusement intensifying exponentially over the course of the next several moments. The force of it was such that Craig's ribs started to ache. Even as this was happening, he knew the outburst was way out of proportion to the actual hilarity level in Bill's comment, which was mild.

But he understood it.

It was a necessary release of tension.

They'd just about wound down from their laughing fit by the time Stacy finally arrived with the drinks. She came bearing a tray loaded up with more booze than seemed appropriate for just three people. Included were multiple beers, a tumbler filled with what was probably Jack and Coke, and multiple shots of some clear liquor. Of the beers, just one was identifiable on sight, High Life in a bottle with a lime wedge floating in it. Intended for Stacy, no doubt, just like the J&C.

The other beers were in pint glasses filled to the foamy brim, one so dark it was almost black. That was almost certainly for Bill, knowing his long-standing preference for Guinness. The third beer had a dark golden-amber hue.

Looking at it, Craig frowned.

He didn't yet know what it was, but one thing was certain—that was not the PBR he'd requested.

Stacy set the tray in the center of the table, pulled up a chair, and started passing the drinks around. The High Life and J&C for herself, just as he'd guessed, the probable pint of Guinness got set in front of Bill, and, no surprise, the mystery golden-amber beer was for him. Right away, his nostrils twitched at the beer's pungent scent, which was of a type he most associated with imperial IPAs. After she was done doling out the beers, Stacy passed out the shots.

Holding her shot glass between slender fingers, Stacy grinned around at them, eyes twinkling with mild drunkenness in the low lighting. "A toast! Here's to seeing the fuckin' Lords again. Who would've thought it?"

Bill chuckled as he picked up his shot. "Not me. Damn near fainted when I saw that flyer. Thought I was hallucinating."

Stacy extended her arm over the table. "Drink, fuckers."

The last thing Craig wanted was to start slamming shots. Too much potential to go down a dangerous road. Whatever proof this mystery liquor was, it sure as shit was a leap beyond nursing weak beers. But now Bill was also holding his glass out toward the center of the table, and they were both watching him in expectation. Refusing to join the toast wasn't a real option. It was just one shot, and he wasn't the heedless kid he'd been, prone to getting carried away. He was a grownup well aware of his limits. After these drinks, he'd put his foot down. No more once they were down the hatch.

Craig lifted his glass and extended it toward the others.

They clinked glasses and tossed back the shots in the only acceptable rock and roll way, knocked back in one swift gulp.

Craig grimaced as the liquid burned the back of his throat.

Tequila.

There was no mistaking that shit for anything else, having experienced more than his fair share of cheap tequila hangovers back in the day.

Like the others, he slapped his empty shot glass down on the table. Hard. A gesture that was almost muscle memory. The stamp of certain ritualistic habits were indelible, even long abandoned ones.

That done, he eyed the dark golden-amber beer in front of him with trepidation. Then he looked at Stacy. "This isn't PBR."

She grinned around the little red cocktail straw clenched between her teeth, chuckling audibly even as she sucked down half the drink in one go. "Nope. It ain't."

Craig sighed. "What is it, then?"

He already had a general idea but wanted her to say it.

She sucked down the last of the J&C, set the rocks glass down with only slightly less force than the shot glass, and picked up her High Life. "I asked the barkeep for the highest fuckin' ABV beer in the joint and he poured me that. It's a double IPA of some kind. A 10.5 percenter."

Craig groaned.

Bill laughed. "Brother, this is what comes of planting dangerous knowledge in the head of a known demoness."

Stacy cackled.

Craig just shook his head.

The beer wasn't much stronger than the imperial IPAs he'd had at dinner earlier, but the issue was piling more strong intoxicants on top of the ones already circulating in his system. Intoxicants which, by the way, had played a lead role in their recent flirtation with mortality.

This is lunacy, he thought. *Just nurse it. Make it last for the next hour at least.*

He could do that. He'd done it many times over the course of the responsible adult phase of his life, which had long ago surpassed his reckless young man phase in duration.

He picked up the glass and brought it close to his mouth, holding it under his nose for another sniff at that strong aroma. Grunting, he put the glass to his lips and took a tentative sip. Then he took a bigger one, rolling the beer around in his mouth as he savored the complex flavor.

He swallowed and set the glass down. "My God, that is a magnificent fucking beer. Absolute nectar of the gods. What is it called?"

He picked up the glass again before Stacy could answer, drinking more.

Stacy shrugged. "Don't know. Like I said, I just asked for the strongest one. You can get the name when you buy the next round."

Craig frowned at the dwindling contents of his glass. He'd already knocked back more than a third of the unknown beer, despite his intentions. "This should be my last. I can't get too fucked up. You know that."

Stacy only grinned in her standard sly way.

Craig's glass was empty less than ten minutes later.

Because of course it fucking was.

He thought about how early it still was. The mopey-looking guys in Wings of Smoke were only just now about done clearing the stage of their shit. The Bile Lords crew still needed to come on and set up their shit, which meant showtime was still maybe a half-hour away, a bit later than scheduled. Then who knew how long they'd play.

He stared at his empty glass and thought some more, this time about the steely glares and sullen silences Janine would subject him to if he returned home later than planned or drunker than he should be.

Going out for an evening of entertainment and drinks wasn't ordinarily an issue in his marriage, perhaps because he did it only rarely and almost never had more than two beers when he did. Coming home mildly buzzed wasn't a big deal, even if Janine wasn't crazy about it. Coming home tanked after seeing a rock show at some seedy club with Bill might be a different story. She was fine with him having the occasional outing with people from work because they were safe. His old friends, though, the ones with whom he shared a long and sordid history of being the *opposite* of safe and responsible . . . well, it was fair to say she didn't care for them at all. Not to the point where she would forbid him to see them. They were long-married adults, after all. He could do as he wanted, within reason.

Could that change or become more of a point of contention if he allowed things to slide just a little bit out of control this one time?

Maybe.

The question facing him was whether it'd be worth a little extra temporary friction at home to let loose a little just this one time?

Maybe. Then again, maybe not. And goddammit, he hated being this indecisive about what was, in the scheme of things, a minor thing. Getting a little extra drunk and getting in late wasn't in the same ballpark as not coming home at all or being an abusive jerk. Right?

Right.

He was teetering right on the edge of a decision when a camera shutter sound made him look up from his empty glass. Stacy was aiming her phone at him. She smirked as she brought the phone closer to her face and started tapping away with her thumbs, typing something.

"What are you doing?"

Her smirking gaze stayed on the phone as she said, "You can't go to a rock show in the modern era without doing a little social media documentation to prove you were there."

Craig made a panicked grab for her phone. "Don't post that!"

She laughed as she jerked it away from him, finished typing her post, and set the phone face-down on the table. "Too late. Already done."

Craig snatched her phone up and saw that her Instagram app was still open, with her post right at the top. He cringed when he saw the unflattering picture, which again brought home how much older he was than the kids hanging out in front of the stage, but also the yellow-tinged lighting made him appear especially bleary-eyed. His gray hair was tousled from the stiff breeze they'd encountered in the parking lot, making him look disheveled in the manner of a monster movie mad scientist. Seeing the bit of spittle on his bottom lip in high-definition didn't help matters, nor did the "humorous" caption about the dangers of rocking out with your cock out as a senior citizen. Just as incriminating was the succession of hashtags about being at the Bile Lords show.

"How do I delete this?"

Stacy snatched the phone back and stuffed it deep inside her purse, which sat open on the edge of the table. "You don't. I can post what I want, fucker. What's the big deal?"

Craig shook his head and squirmed a bit in his seat, his agitation level increasing as he clenched his fists and glared at her.

Bill wiped his lips after taking a sip of Guinness and answered for him. "Come on, Stacy. Think about it."

Her expression was one of clueless confusion before awareness dawned, signaled by a narrowing of her eyes and a twitch of her bottom lip. "Oh, Craig. Jesus. You didn't tell Janine I'd be with you guys. Did you?"

Craig's silence was the only answer necessary.

Stacy made a sound of deep annoyance as she agitatedly dug her phone back out of the purse, stabbed her finger hard at the screen a few times, and dumped the phone on the table. "Fine. I deleted it. Happy?"

Rather than answering, Craig pushed his chair back, grabbed the drink tray and his empty glass, heaved himself up with a loud grunt of effort and a flare of aching bones, and stalked his way over to the bar.

Once he was able to squeeze into a spot between stools, he had a conversation with the bartender and determined that the beer he'd had was something called a Bloody Chainsaw double IPA from Cursed Moonlight Brewing. In the course of this conversation, he also learned that, in addition to standard pints, the draft beers on tap at the Skull Spark Club were available in a twenty-ounce size. He ordered a tall glass of Bloody Chainsaw and some other drinks and carried them to the table on the same tray Stacy had used to transport the first round.

It was Stacy's turn to eye the drinks in a dubious way before meeting Craig's jittery gaze. "I can see you're upset," she said, in a calm tone absent any trace of her previous manic prickliness. "Maybe sit and think a few minutes before you start down this road."

That was rich, coming from her.

Craig's only response was a derisive little snort.

"Okay, avoidance. Everything old is new again." Stacy snagged the new bottle of High Life he'd delivered and looked away. "Whatever, you moody little shit."

Craig ignored the digs, knowing they weren't unearned.

Up on the stage, roadies for the Bile Lords had started setting up the band's gear. There were just two of them, a pair of heavily tattooed guys with shaggy, dyed black hair. One was rail-skinny, the other not exactly fat, but a bit pudgy around the middle. The slightly thicker one looked significantly older than his work partner. Unlike the departed members of Wings of Smoke, these guys went about their work in a methodical, all business way, working fast, but taking care to make sure everything was done right.

At least that was how it appeared to Craig as he half-watched while doling out the rest of the drinks, including another round of tequila shots. The older roadie looked sort of like a professional burnout, like maybe he'd worked with the band going back to their glory days, a rock and roll loyalist who lived for the road.

Craig took a big sip from his second beer and nodded toward the stage. "It's sort of fucked up seeing them like this. Some dumpy out-of-the-way place in a nothing little town like Drayton fucking Falls. You guys remember when we saw them at Headley Auditorium on the *Babylon* tour? Us and 12,000 other rowdy-ass motherfuckers screaming loud enough to shake the rafters?" He took a bigger gulp of beer and shook his head. "Hard to believe we're seeing that same band in this shithole."

Neither of his friends responded right away, nor did they immediately reach for their new tequila shots.

On the stage, one of the roadies strummed a guitar, some chords from a punk song they all recognized. Not a Bile Lords original, but it'd been on *Covered In Filth*, a covers album the band did as their initial wave of popularity waned with the rise of grunge. A fun and raw album of snotty songs, it'd marked the permanent end of the band's classic original lineup. The roadie paused before strumming the same chords again, then he shouted something at his younger colleague, who was on his knees at the back of stage, fiddling with wires and equipment.

Stacy glanced at the stage. "Shit, even their gear looks secondhand. The kids up their earlier had better stuff. Are we sure we're seeing the actual Bile Lords and not some half-assed tribute band?"

Craig frowned. "It's them. I mean, I'm pretty sure. This gig is listed in the tour section of the band's official site. I know you looked at that, right?"

Stacy shrugged. "Just that one time when you bugged me to check it out. Looked kind of shit. Like something a teenager would put together." She considered what she'd said and added, "A dumb one, I mean. Not one of those tech geniuses like so many of them seem to be now."

Bill laughed. "We would've called them nerds in our day. In the passe derogatory sense."

"Did you click on the music tab?" Craig asked, still looking right at Stacy. "That was the clincher for me. Erased any authenticity doubt."

One of Stacy's eyebrows went up. "How so?"

Craig smiled for the first time since returning from the bar. "There was a snippet of a new single. Kyle Bile on vocals, for sure. Impossible to mistake that voice for anyone else."

Stacy looked askance at him. "Really? A new Lords song? Their first in, what . . . over ten years? And you're just now mentioning it?"

Reaching for his beer, Craig nodded. "Yeah. It's . . . okay. I guess."

Stacy snatched up her phone again, swiped at the screen, and did a quick bit of thumb-tapping. "Well, damn. You weren't lying."

She pressed the volume button, raising it to its highest level, and the three of them leaned over the table as they listened to the snippet, which ran just over a minute.

No one rendered an immediate verdict.

Bill was the first to lean back again, his gaze flicking toward Craig as he said, "You were wrong. That song isn't 'okay'. It kind of . . . sucks."

Stacy added, "It's so generic. He's right about one thing, though. No mistaking that voice. That's definitely Kyle."

She reached for the shot glass Craig had set in front of her several minutes earlier and tossed the tequila down her throat.

The three of them sat in bummed-out silence for a bit, Craig thinking back to his initial middling response to the song. He'd listened to the snippet just that one time before now, in what he retroactively understood was a more receptive, noncritical mindset, his enthusiasm for the upcoming show perhaps disengaging the analytical part of his brain. Hearing it again in the company of these old friends was another story. It was a reset, like truly hearing it for the first time.

Stacy was right. It was generic. And that was about the best you could say about it.

"What happened to them?" She made a scoffing sound, glancing again at the stage. "Wasn't it only a decade ago they had that resurgence? Had a big hit and were back to touring arenas?"

Bill nodded. "Yeah, 2015. I saw them at that new arena in Breckenridge. You guys couldn't go for . . . reasons. Whatever excuses you had at the time."

Craig grimaced. "I admit I was maybe a little snobbish about it. Thought I'd become too mature for 80s sleaze rock. Regretted it later. As you know."

"I don't even remember," Stacy said, shrugging. "That was around the time of my divorce. Shit got fucked up for a while. The point stands. How could they have fallen so far since then?"

Craig drank more of his beer. "I don't know. To be honest, I haven't kept up with news in the rock world much at all in a long time. I do know that resurgence didn't last long at all, like barely even into the next year."

Bill said, "Also, to old fucks like us, a decade doesn't seem like that long ago, but really, it's been a while."

A glum, mostly silent mood began to pervade again. They all started paying more attention to their phones, lapsing into nursing the beers like the old people they were instead of chugging them. At one point, Craig noticed that a young woman in tight black leather pants and a cropped Bile Lords shirt had started setting up a merch table. Like the roadies, her hair was dyed black and cut in a similarly choppy, punkish style. She was setting up well away from the stage, the cafeteria-style table positioned to the left of a short hallway that led to the bathrooms.

Speaking of which . . .

Craig downed the rest of his beer, guzzling fast again, then pushed back the chair and rose creakily to his feet. "Gotta hit the head."

He'd taken hardly more than a step away from the table when Stacy followed his lead and fell into step next to him, leaning close to say, "Saw you staring at the merch chick. She's hot shit. You can't hit on her, though. You'll gross her out."

Craig smiled. "Sweet talker. I remember when all you did was tell me how hot for me you were."

Stacy smirked, not without affection. "Yeah, and you're still kind of handsome for an old fuck, but this chick will take one look at you and see her father. Shit, more like her grandfather, now that I think of it. But, hell, who knows, maybe she'll be all torn up with daddy issues, in which case anything's possible."

Craig winced. "No thank you. I've got enough problems in my life without adding anything as messy as that to the mix. Anyway, I really did just get up to piss. No point in even checking out the merch. None of that shit will fit me. I don't know if you've noticed, but I don't exactly have a rock and roll body these days."

"I do, though."

Craig gave her a sidelong glance, looking her up and down.

"Can't disagree there."

As they reached the hallway, Stacy veered over to the merch table and started talking up the girl behind it while Craig continued on toward the bathrooms. The door to the one-person capacity men's room was open a crack. He knocked and pushed the door open a bit wider when there wasn't a response, then stepped in when he saw it was unoccupied, closing and locking the door behind him. He'd been in some nasty bathrooms before, most often at gas stations in remote places, the kind you sometimes had no choice but to use on long road trips when viable stopping places along the way were few and far between. Places where there was piss all over the floor and the one toilet was hopelessly clogged with what looked like an entire roll of toilet paper or more, sometimes with a pile of shit on top.

The men's bathroom at Skull Spark wasn't as dire as that, but it was far from sparkling and pristine. While the toilet wasn't clogged, an old plunger with a wood handle resting next to it suggested that was sometimes an issue. Unfortunately, there *was* some piss on the floor and along one side of the closed toilet seat. Not a full-on pond of it like he'd encountered at a few of the viler of those rural gas station restrooms, but enough to dissuade any notion of touching the thing with his fingers or bare bottom.

Taking care not to get his shoes wet with some drunk asshole's urine, he approached the toilet and raised the lid with the tip of his shoe. It was a familiar maneuver from days gone by, one that wasn't as easy to execute, thanks to having a gut these days, but with a bit of strain while wobbling precariously for a moment on one leg, he got it done. Then he unzipped, took the works out, and unleashed a heavy stream of beer water, aka piss. What was that thing his dad always used to say about booze?

Oh, yeah.

You don't really buy liquor or beer, you rent it.

As the heavy rush of his stream continued, he looked around at the walls in the cramped space, which were covered in graffiti. Here was another thing that hadn't changed at all since his days of patronizing this place in its previous incarnation. The graffiti was so dense, more of the faded old ink was visible than white paint, especially in the areas right around the toilet. Some of the writing had been rendered in large, stylized letters, while other messages and slogans were so small they were almost microscopic. They'd been inscribed on the walls all sorts of ways—straight across, upside down, sideways, in drunken swirls and loops, with some of the tinier messages inside the closed parts of larger letters. A fair portion had been scratched over or were too blurred to read.

Taken as a whole, the graffiti was like an ever-mutating piece of profane art, an organic collaboration perpetuated down through the years and decades by people who never knew each other, quite a few of them likely dead. If he cared to take the time to examine the sloppy inscriptions more closely, he might even find a few things he'd written, but it'd take a long time and wasn't worth the trouble. His stream had slowed to a trickle and he needed to get back to his friends. The ongoing work of the roadies was audible in the bathroom. The thump of drums, the thrum of the bass, and more chugging guitar chords, so much of it he knew time was growing short. He'd been to a lot of rock shows in dinky little clubs and knew what it sounded like when the setup phase was getting into its final stages.

He was shaking off the last droplets of piss and preparing to zip up when, out of nowhere, or perhaps at some subtle subconscious prompt, he turned his head sharply to the left and squinted as he leaned in that direction, his eyes zooming in on a particular inscription like a movie camera doing a dramatic sudden closeup shot.

Stacy 4-ever.

His handwriting.

Seeing this made him feel dizzy, causing him to stagger and step into the little puddle of piss next to the toilet. He scowled and immediately stepped back, shaking the liquid from his shoe. Once he had his feet more firmly under him, he allowed himself another, longer look at the unexpected glimpse into his distant past. Once upon a time, probably well over thirty years ago, he'd held his hand and a pen to that section of wall and scrawled those words there. It was like a message from a ghost of his old self, a telegram from the past.

A painful reminder that, in fact, nothing is forever.

Not even love.

Fuck. I need to get out of here.

He stepped over to the sink and turned the water on to wash his hands. He'd just pumped some of the liquid soap from the dispenser when someone rapped hard on the door.

He cleared his throat and raised his voice so it could be heard over what the roadies were doing. "*Almost done! Be out in a second!*"

After lathering his hands and running them under the water, he tore off some brown paper towels from the wall dispenser, quickly dried his hands, and dropped the crumpled wet towels in an overflowing trash receptacle. An unexpected roadblock stood in his way when he finally opened the door.

Stacy.

She peered in at him, a look of impatience on her face. Before he could say anything or step out into the hallway, she put a hand against his chest and pushed him back inside.

She closed the door and locked it.

Confusion was soon replaced by apprehension. Fuzzy memories of wildly impulsive things they'd done when they'd been together swirled through his head, internal alarm bells clanging. He backed away from her with careless haste, the heel of a shoe stepping in the piss puddle.

He was no longer the heedless young man who sometimes did dumb, thoughtless things that hurt people he cared about. He wasn't about to transgress against his marriage, whatever Stacy's intentions were here. Knowing this didn't change how off-kilter he felt, how vulnerable. They shouldn't be in this private space together, he and this old flame whose very existence got under his wife's skin. Never mind secretly being at a show with her, Janine would prefer he cut off all ties with her forever, including social media connections. Hell, he knew the only reason Janine followed Stacy on Instagram was to spy, to watch for any hints of anything even slightly suggestive of misbehavior.

And it was crazy. He knew that, too.

In a truly healthy marriage, a spouse wouldn't be so obsessed with a partner's old relationship that'd ended a third of a fucking century ago.

Okay, yes, it was a bit fucked up, but . . .

Stacy rolled her eyes. "Jesus Christ, will you please relax?"

Craig frowned. "What do you mean?"

She smirked. "I can almost see your thoughts dancing in little bubbles over your head like in a comic book. We're not gonna fuck in this disgusting hole, okay? That's not why I've cornered you in here."

Craig willed his nerves to settle. "Okay. Why, then? The only other reason you'd do this is if you've got something to say you don't want to say in front of Bill."

She grunted. "Bill means well, but if he heard any of this, he'd just give us that patented disapproving look of his and start dispensing worldly advice from his somehow more enlightened perspective."

Craig laughed. "Yeah. Okay. I know the look you mean. You've got a point."

Stacy nodded. "And we don't have long before he starts suspecting we're doing exactly what you thought I had in mind. So tell the truth without mincing a single fucking word. Why did you let your wife think I wouldn't be with you guys tonight? I mean, it's been a while, but it's not like we've never hung out."

Craig's face contorted subtly in a way that hinted at complicated and ancient sources of pain. Stacy could probably guess most of it, but she'd asked him to say it, so he did. "Janine was never part of our group. She came into my life right after we all started drifting apart. Early on, we had that interrogation new couples eventually put each other through, that thorough inventory of romantic histories. She knows how I felt about you, how breaking up almost destroyed me."

Obvious anger flared in Stacy's expression. "Destroyed *you?*"

Craig held up a placating hand. "Both of us. I know. I fucking *know*. We were both assholes, but I was the bigger one. By far. The point is, Janine has always known I never felt as intensely about her as I did about you. I love her, I do. I love the life we've had. The daughter we raised. But that burning passion, that tragic fucking Romeo and Juliet thing . . . she and I never had that. And . . . well, she resents it. Resents *you*."

They stared at each other close to a minute without speaking.

The silence ended when someone banged on the door.

A corner of Stacy's mouth twitched in rage. She turned her head and screamed at the top of her lungs. "*Use the ladies' room, motherfucker!*"

In the hallway, a male voice muttered something indistinct after a stunned pause, but there was no repeat of the knock.

Stacy was calmer when she looked at Craig again, but a disquieting intensity lingered in her demeanor. She raised a finger, shaking it at him. "Until you have the guts to leave her, which you should probably do if things between you are as dysfunctional as they fucking sound, don't ever lie to her again about seeing me. You know how I feel about shit like that."

Her eyes brimmed with sudden tears.

Craig's mouth opened in helpless dismay, but she was already turning away from him.

She unlocked and hauled the door open, disappearing into the hallway.

A moment later, he pushed the door shut again and locked it. Not because he wished to delay the awkwardness of returning to the table to sit with her again after that impassioned speech—at least not entirely for that reason—but because the need to piss had built back up.

He sighed.

Another of the endless hazards of growing old.

He took another leak, washed his hands again, and finally walked out of the bathroom.

As Craig came out of the hallway, he saw that the size of the crowd in front of the stage had increased noticeably in the several minutes that had passed since he'd last glimpsed it. A portion of the older segment of the audience appeared to have risen from their tables to join the other standing spectators.

This kept him from seeing that someone else had joined his

friends at their table until he was most of the way there. The stranger's back was turned toward him, which prevented him from recognizing the man at first glance. He noted with gratitude that he'd pulled up a chair from another table instead of taking his unoccupied spot, meaning Stacy or Bill had told him it was already taken. Not a big thing, but he liked the idea of his friends looking out for him like that.

He'd just about arrived at the table when he caught a glimpse of the man's profile and realized he'd seen him before, though really the backwards Bile Lords ballcap should have given it away already. This was the wiry older guy he'd noticed during the opening band's performance.

Craig was certain he'd never seen him before tonight. Why he was at their table was a somewhat irksome mystery. This was a resurfacing of his old antisocial streak, a trait he'd worked to train out of himself over the years, but in this case he couldn't help it. Even without having spoken to the man, he had a vague sense of something off-putting about him, a sketchiness that stirred instant distrust.

Stacy caught Craig's eye as he began to move around the table, and he perceived a guardedness in her expression. It was possible this was misperception, a case of him projecting his own feelings onto her. She might be trying to communicate something else to him, some warning to keep things light and reserve further discussion of the things they'd talked about in the bathroom for some other day and time.

A day he knew might never come.

Because right now they both had a fair amount of alcohol floating through their systems. Tomorrow, in the cold, sober light of day, they might each regret having said certain things. He knew from too much past experience that sometimes it was easier to just let such things slide. It wasn't that real issues had not been raised but more that those issues were too delicate and potentially devastating to ever solve. Because sometimes, maybe in particular for people as old as they were with such complicated histories, it really was better to let sleeping dogs lie forever.

He wished he and Stacy had never split.

Wished he'd never fucked her half-sister.

Wished he'd never been such a worthless fucking asshole when he was young.

Wished a lot of goddamn things.

But . . .

It's too late for us. That chapter is finished, left behind too long ago, the whole sad story already entering its final pages.

Lord, that was maudlin as hell.

Maybe he'd had too much to drink already. Probably, yeah.

But then, as he dropped into his chair, and scooted it toward the table, he saw that a new tall glass of what he assumed was Bloody Chainsaw double IPA was in front of him. He eyed it with trepidation, knowing he was already right on the edge of true drunkenness. And knowing that twenty more ounces of so strong a concoction might push him all the way over that edge.

What was he going to do, though? Refuse it?

He sighed.

Of course not.

He picked up the glass and brought it to his mouth, taking a long swig as the taste confirmed his guess about the type of beer. A sound of profound appreciation escaped his lips as he returned the glass to the table. The taste was so rich and satisfying that the briefly entertained notion of refusing it now struck him as the height of absurdity. What kind of fool refused something of such quality?

A smart one, an inner voice said.

Which was immediately countered by a secondary voice that said, *Shut the fuck up*.

He cleared his throat and nodded toward the beer. "Needed that."

His assumption was that Bill had picked up this round, but Stacy said, "You can thank . . . Rodney, was it?"

She lifted a fresh Jack and Coke and made a toasting gesture.

Craig looked straight at the stranger for the first time. From this closer vantage point, he looked even older than he'd originally perceived, the many sharp age lines etched in the rawhide flesh looking like they'd been carved with a knife. In that first instant of direct eye contact, the man's expression struck him as cold and flinty. Then he grinned, exposing rows of tobacco-stained teeth with more than a few gaps, eyes lighting up with an apparent warmness that somewhat dispelled Craig's first impression.

He extended a hand across the table. "Rodney Cantor. Pleased to meet."

Craig shook the man's hand, noting the calloused roughness of his strong grip. "Likewise."

Rodney settled into his seat.

Stacy looked at Craig, an eyebrow quirked. "Rodney here works for the Bile Lords. So he says."

Craig looked the man over again, reassessing him in this new context. He decided it made sense. Here was another old road dog, like the portlier of the two roadies still up there on the stage.

"Is that so? How long you been with them?"

Rodney grinned again. "God's honest truth, friend. I've worked with Kyle going all the way back to the beginning, just about. If you pull up the video for 'Locked and Loaded', you can see a much younger version of my handsome mug. I'm only in there for a hot second, but you can freeze it and see me there plain as day."

Stacy picked up her phone and leaned toward Craig, angling it so he could see the screen, where she'd already pulled up the video in question, cued up to the spot. She tapped it so it could play for a moment, then paused it.

Craig leaned closer.

Then he grunted. "I'll be damned. That *is* you."

Rodney nodded. "Told ya."

After a glance toward the stage, Craig said, "What do you do for the band these days?"

Rodney sipped from a bottle of Coors Banquet, wiped his lips. "I did the roadie thing for a long time, over forty damn years, and truth is, at seventy-one, my body just ain't up to it anymore. Bending down, stooping over, lifting and moving heavy shit, all that kind of thing would fuck me up if I tried to do it as much as the job requires. Which is why I'm not up there on the stage getting my hands dirty. These days I'm more like a road mascot and occasional troubleshooter. Bit of a charity case, if I'm being honest. Kyle just likes me being around. He finds my presence . . . reassuring."

Craig reached for his glass. "Yeah? That's interesting. I guess there's a lot of value in having a trusted face around through all the changes in the band."

Rodney nodded, pointing an index finger at Craig. "Nailed it, brother. Loyalty and dependability, that's what I bring to the table."

Bill, who sat nearest the former roadie, nudged him with an elbow. "You haven't heard the best part yet. Rodney says if we can hang around a while after the show, he can take us in to see Kyle, sort of a private meet-and-greet thing."

Craig's eyebrows went up. "Oh, shit. Really? That'd be cool."

Rodney finished his beer and pushed his chair back. "If I'm lyin', I'm dyin'. Y'all just stick around and I'll take care of ya. Might have to hang out as much as a half hour after the show's done before the man himself will see you."

He was up and gone before they could say anything else.

Craig frowned as he watched the man disappear through the loose knot of standing spectators. While the idea of a private meeting with an artist he'd idolized in his youth excited him even as a jaded old man, the prospect of further delaying his return home was troubling. What bothered him most was the unscheduled, casual nature of the proposed meeting. The old roadie's estimate of the post-show wait time might not be accurate. He'd said a half-hour, but what if it dragged on for an hour or longer?

Then there was the question of how long the meeting itself would last. If it was just a quick exchange of greetings along with signing some autographs, that might be okay, but what if it turned into a real hangout that just went on and on?

He hated to voice it to his friends, but the reality was he'd have to clear a delay of that indefinite potential length with Janine before committing to it.

Stacy sighed. "If it gets too late for you, Bill and I will just Uber home. You don't need to sweat it."

Craig grimaced.

She'd sensed exactly what he was thinking, like always, in that cliched way long-term married couples often do. Only they weren't a couple and hadn't spent prolonged periods of time together in many years. It was scary to think how advanced that telepathy-like intuition would be by now if they'd never split.

Craig picked up his phone and held it in his lap, frowning as he stared at the screen, stomach twisting in knots as he pondered how to word the text he needed to send. "Maybe I'll just see how things go, make up my mind later."

Bill drained off the last of his latest pint, then he pushed his chair back and rose to his feet, wobbling slightly from all the beer he'd had.

"I'm off to the little boys' room. Show's about to start, looks like. Don't want to feel like my bladder's about to explode when it does."

Craig frowned.

He was already feeling a bit of a renewed urge to go again, speaking of strained bladders.

Fucking beer. Fucking old age. Fucking obligations. Christ.

He picked up his glass and brought it to his mouth as Bill walked away. Tilting his head back, he took several big gulps, downing almost half the remaining beer before setting the glass on the table again.

Stacy was staring at him.

Craig wiped his mouth and groaned. "What?"

She grunted. "You're all worked up. Probably making yourself sick."

"What about it?" he asked, snapping at her.

Stacy rolled her eyes. "Don't take that tone with me. You sound like a whiny-ass little kid." She shook her head, expression softening. "It's not worth it, Craig. Just go home after the show. Bill and I will be fine. And you won't have to be so damn miserable."

Craig frowned. "I'm gonna send her a text. Explain how this is a once-in-a-lifetime thing. She's an adult. She'll understand."

He tapped his phone and brought it closer to his face to unlock it. Before he could send a message to Janine, he saw he already had a text from her.

The dramatic way his face changed when he looked at the message and saw what his wife had sent prompted multiple worried inquiries from Stacy while he sat there with his mouth hanging open, staring in stunned disbelief at the phone.

What he was looking at was a photo she'd sent nearly half an hour earlier. It was a screenshot of Stacy's deleted Instagram post. She'd included a caption of an angry face emoji and the words, "This you?"

Stacy scooted her chair closer and began to lean toward him, angling for a glimpse of what had upset him.

Craig turned his phone off before she could get a look, sliding it into his hip pocket before picking up his beer glass again.

Stacy made an exasperated sound and leaned back. "That bad, huh?"

He drained his glass and said nothing for a stretch of moments, not looking at her, staring into an unfocused point straight ahead, where people moved in and out of his field of vision as he took no note of them or anything else. His stomach wasn't twisting itself in knots anymore. On a physical level, he felt more relaxed than at any point since he had entered the club, but that wasn't the same thing as feeling good. He felt like a pit had opened inside him, a black hole abyss into which his life as he'd known it for so long was threatening to slide, to be devoured and perhaps disappear forever.

As he sat there without speaking or reacting for so long, Stacy became steadily more agitated, leaning close again to grip him by the shoulder and shake him. She yelled at him, but to his ears it was white noise.

He pushed away from the table and stood up.

By that point, Bill was on his way back, had nearly reached the table again when he took note of Craig's demeanor, casting a wary glance Stacy's way as he said, "What's happening? Is he all right?"

Stacy snorted. "Who can tell? He's apparently lost the ability to speak."

Craig looked from Stacy to Bill and back again. "I'm going to the bar. Back in a minute."

He turned away from them, navigated his way around the rail, and approached the bar, which was emptying out some as more people headed toward the floor in anticipation of the show beginning. After putting in the order for more drinks, he thought of the phone in his pocket and the damning screenshot he could see again if he turned it back on.

He was still in shock.

An argument could be made that he shouldn't be surprised. Janine's resentment of Stacy wasn't a new thing. He'd been upset when Stacy posted the picture for good reason, but because she'd deleted it within just a couple of minutes, he'd believed it wouldn't be a problem.

That his wife had been looking at the Instagram account of a woman she hated within that exact narrow window of time, at just the right instant to glimpse something so potentially world-upending, boggled his mind. He couldn't believe it'd happened. It spoke to a level of obsession so all-encompassing he found it disturbing. It suggested the bond they had was fundamentally damaged in a way he'd never grasped, further suggested they'd only been going through the semi-comfortable motions for a long time for no reason other than apathy or inertia.

Craig carried the new round of drinks to the table. He set the tray down and remained standing as Stacy directed her piercing, perceptive gaze at him. Reaching into his pocket, he took out his phone and powered it on. Then he opened the text window and showed her what was there.

She took the phone from him and stared at it for a long moment.

Then she handed it back to him and said, "Okay."

Her voice was monotone, as devoid of inflection as he'd ever heard it.

Craig dropped the phone back in his pocket and headed off to the bathroom. This time it was occupied and he had to wait in the hallway a few minutes, listening to the growing buzz from the crowd, which was displaced by cheers and whistles as a recorded piece of intro music played. He felt like he was lost in space, in a trance, mind numb, body on the verge of floating away.

He finally got into the bathroom just as the recorded intro was nearing its end. Standing shakily in front of the toilet while he urinated, he soon heard a muffled hum of amplifiers, followed by a cymbal-crashing drum roll. The show was starting. He was still watching his piss patter into the toilet. A familiar voice screamed into a microphone as he imagined himself falling into the toilet and disappearing down the drain, becoming a boneless mass of goo and slush sliding down into the sewer to mix with the shit and other forms of waste, down deep into the disgusting muck of filth where he belonged.

Out on the stage, Kyle Bile's amplified voice was asking Drayton Falls if it was ready to rock. The enthusiastic audience response was far more robust than the earlier vibe of tired apathy. There were loud cheers and even a few high-pitched screams and whistles.

Craig finally stumbled out of the bathroom shortly after the band launched into "Locked and Loaded", making the curious choice to begin the set with the biggest song from their early heyday.

As he came out of the hallway, he saw that the size of the crowd was about triple what it'd been for the opening band, yet the space in front of the stage was still far from congested. He was able to locate Bill and Stacy within seconds, standing right up front with beers in hand, and the ample room to move around allowed him to make his way over to them without having to aggressively jostle his way there. He'd had harder times making it to the counter at Starbucks on really busy days.

Bill spotted him first, raising a tall can of PBR in salute. He nudged Stacy, who turned toward him with a grin as she bobbed her head along to the hard-rocking groove of the song. She waved with one hand, rocking back on her heels as she guzzled from a High Life bottle with the other. Taking a quick glance around as he stepped into place alongside her, he spotted some of the young people he'd seen watching Wings of Smoke, but that element of the crowd was vastly outnumbered by all the AARP-eligible gray-haired types. He took particular note of that one really drunk young girl he'd seen earlier, the one who'd looked like she was about to fall over unconscious. She'd disappeared for a while but was back again, standing right at the edge of the stage and staring up at Kyle Bile in a way that was either sheer, mindless adoration or a reflection of how high she was.

Or both.

"Locked and Loaded" came to a crashing, energetic end about a minute and a half after Craig had made his way up front. The volume of the cheer that rose up belied the modest size of the crowd. Stacy raised her High Life bottle high into the air and unleashed a scream that made her sound like the wild teenaged rock and roller she'd been when he first met her. Hearing it sent a thrill of excitement through him which, along with all the alcohol he'd consumed, allowed him to forget his life might be on the verge of falling apart.

On the stage, Kyle staggered away from the microphone and just managed to avoid tripping over a cable as he snagged a bottle of whiskey from a corner of the drum riser. As he brought the bottle to his mouth and upended it, the drummer began belting out a steady, rhythmic beat. The bass player joined in within moments, the combined thrum of the rhythm section making Craig's body feel like it was vibrating. One of the two young guitarists filling in for the band's original six-stringers stepped to the edge of the stage, struck a classic rock and roll pose, legs spread wide with guitar slung low, and added chugging, crunchy chords. The other guitarist, the lead player, launched into a solo, tearing off a lengthy sequence of blistering notes.

The only original member of the Bile Lords on this stage was Kyle, which possibly explained why this iteration of the band wasn't playing larger venues. His younger hired guns had the look down and were skilled enough to convincingly replicate the original lineup's sound, but the vibe was basically enthusiastic kids jamming with their drunk uncle. Because that's what this was, a jam to fill time while the singer slugged back a truly absurd amount of hard liquor.

Craig idly wondered whether it was truly whiskey in that bottle. Maybe it was flat Coke or tea, as he'd heard certain singers from back in the day would drink to get a rise out of the audience.

He soon dismissed the idea. Kyle didn't look like a guy who was faking severe alcoholism. He was bloated and sweaty, swaying on his feet in a way that didn't look at all like an act. The black leather pants and sleeveless black vest he wore looked too tight, straining against his bulk. It was shocking how bad he looked, this being a man who was once one of the top hard rock heartthrobs. His sculpted physique and smoldering good looks had inspired lust in countless legions of women and young girls, with his face pasted on the covers of so many magazines in those days. *Hit Parader* and *Circus. Creem, Rip, Spin, and Rolling Stone.* Even *Entertainment Weekly* and *Newsweek* toward the end of 1989, signaling a temporary full embracement by mainstream media.

Kyle at last returned the nearly depleted liquor bottle to the corner of the drum riser and made his way back to the front of the stage. He gripped the microphone in both hands and bobbed his head to the rocking rhythm, letting his sweaty hair hang over his face. The jam went on for at least another full minute, becoming almost monotonous. Then Kyle's head abruptly snapped up and he screamed into the microphone.

"*Who's ready to get nasty with the motherfucking Bile Lords!?*"

The band ripped into "Nasty Thing".

Something about the manic riffage that powered the song appeared to inject energy into the aging singer. He ran and spun his way across the little stage with the frenzied ferocity of metal singers half his age, somehow miraculously missing that perilous cable every time. Stacy screamed and jumped up and down. She grabbed hold of Craig and shook him hard, eliciting a reluctant smile as some of the sourness and gloom that had crept into his mood began to slip away. Even Bill was swaying and swinging his beer around, singing along at the top of his lungs.

Soon enough, Craig was singing along with them.

As the show went on, Kyle's renewed energy persisted, an act of pugnacious defiance against the deterioration of his body and the passage of time. He struck dramatic poses infused with a strong dose of the charisma that had made him a star, howling like a man possessed on their hardest rocking songs. Somehow he kept up with his far younger bandmates, interacting and playing off them, grinning in a half-demented way as they matched his manic energy. The young ones gave no appearance of going through the motions for a payday, looking as completely invested as if they were the founding members.

Even when the band played "I'll See You Again", the one ballad from *Hollywood Babylon*, Kyle delivered, adopting a Jim Morrison-like croon filled with palpable emotion. The cheer that rose up as the final, haunting notes of that one rang out exceeded every previous delirious ovation.

Scanning the crowd yet again at that point, Craig still saw a sea of old faces, but the majority were not behaving like people ready to move into retirement homes. They were rocking out with abandon, not quite recreating the mosh pits of their youths, but throwing their bodies around with heedless gusto, screaming, cheering, crying, throwing hard rock horns in the air, banging heads like it was 1986 instead of 2026. Tomorrow their bodies would ache and complain and generally remind them of the limits of fragile old bones, but right here and now, in these electric moments, no one cared.

Time melted away, seemed to turn backward.

The rest of the world might have moved on from this kind of sleazy hard rock spectacle, but not the people gathered here tonight. These were the true faithful, the most devout of rock and roll acolytes.

The reconstituted Bile Lords played all the big hits and a whole lot of fan favorites that'd never been radio singles. One of the deepest cuts was their version of "Sonic Reducer" by the Dead Boys. Always one of Craig's favorites, its inclusion as part of the band's set was a pleasant surprise, even after hearing that roadie play part of it before the show. By the end of the song, he realized he'd been banging and bobbing his head as energetically as anyone.

Unlike in the big arena show days, there was no break for an encore, just Kyle thanking everyone for coming out and announcing the final song, which turned out to be "The Bad Man", the big comeback single from over a decade ago. The song was delivered with the same passion and conviction as all the preceding numbers, from its slow, ominous beginning and the rousing buildup of the middle sections all the way up to its frenetic conclusion, which the band dragged out to at least twice the length of the recorded version.

When it was done, Kyle stepped back to the microphone, gripped it with the fiery-eyed look of a mad general about to send his troops charging toward certain death, and delivered his final words to the crowd: "*We're the goddamn Bile Lords, and don't you ever fucking forget it! Good fucking night!*"

Then he let go of the microphone and stalked off the stage, the other band members abandoning their instruments and following within seconds to the echo of fading feedback.

Craig stared at the empty stage, ears ringing, body still vibrating with adrenaline, somewhat taken aback by how thoroughly he'd ended up enjoying the show. The declarative way Kyle had bellowed the first word of *We're the goddamn Bile Lords* resonated in particular, like a gauntlet thrown down, a dare or perhaps even a threat to anyone who might say this wasn't the real Bile Lords.

He had to admit now it felt like a valid assertion.

This wasn't the originals. Nothing could ever disguise that or erase what the old band had been to its fans, but it felt more than fair to say this was probably as good as it was ever going to be again, barring an unlikely reunion of the classic lineup.

Stacy grabbed hold of Craig and shook him again as the cheers of the crowd at last began to fade. The huge, unrestrained smile she showed him made her look younger. Not miraculously half-her-age-young, but visibly less aged, enough to feed into that illusion of time turning back.

At least for a fleeting little while.

Stacy shook him yet again. Then she laughed. "Holy shit. Can you believe how fucking great that was?"

Craig shook his head. "I honestly can't. I'm shocked."

He'd thought Kyle might pass out or fall off the stage at the start of the show. That early unsteadiness aside, the singer had put on one of the most thrilling rock and roll frontman performances Craig had ever seen, though he supposed the visceral power of it was magnified somewhat by being so close to the stage. All the previous times they'd seen the Bile Lords it'd been from a much greater distance, with much bigger crowds, but the greatness of tonight's show couldn't be entirely attributed to the intimacy of the setting. Nor, he believed, was his perception of what he'd witnessed a product of having consumed more alcohol at one time than he had in many years. He'd watched the whole show without venturing back to the bar for another drink, allowing his buzz to ebb somewhat. He felt certain an eventual return to full sobriety wouldn't much diminish his impression of what he'd seen, if at all.

Despite Kyle announcing "The Bad Man" as the final song of the night, the crowd lingered in front of the stage for several minutes, staying loud as they cheered and hollered, calling out for an encore. For a little while, Craig thought the band might actually return to the stage, so overwhelming was the sheer volume of the crowd's loud desire for it.

But it didn't happen.

Little by little, the reality that the band would not be taking the stage again sank in for the onlookers, the volume of the cheers and applause slowly fading. At last, a few people began to leave, and as soon as the first fans departed, others followed suit, taking that initial surrender to the inevitable as their signal to go. The exodus then began in earnest, soon leaving the club almost empty.

As groups of people continued to leave, Craig excused himself and made his way back over to the bathroom. He'd watched an entire rock show while holding a full bladder and was in dire need of relief. By the time he returned to the floor in front of the stage, the place was even emptier, almost desolate. Bill and Stacy were still where he'd left them, talking about the show and idly observing as the roadies started breaking down the equipment and working to clear the stage. Craig found the activities of the crew less interesting than he had before the show started, divested as they were of that pre-show sense of anticipation. He felt a little like he used to feel coming down from a drug high, the world around him gray and dull, removed of its gleaming neon sheen.

Some of what he was feeling was rooted in recognition that the show was already on its way to being just another fond memory. Another day would come and then another after that, followed by weeks and months and years, and the visceral thrill and joy of this experience would fade and then disappear.

He hated that, wished he could push that awareness out of his head and just exist in the moment, relish and hold on to the good feelings the experience had inspired, but it was difficult. Snatches of memory from too many shows he'd seen decades ago flitted through his brain, taunting him with reminders that once upon a time he'd felt these same things in the smoky, boozy aftermath of each and every one of them. But time always passed, faster and faster, a whirlwind of years gone by, decades that melted away in what felt like the blink of an eye. He couldn't help wondering how he'd feel about this show in another metaphorical blink of the eye. Another ten years, say. Would he even still be alive by then?

In bygone days, he never had morbid thoughts like these after a show. Rock and roll shows used to make him feel invincible. Immortal, more vibrantly alive, but now he couldn't summon feelings like that no matter how hard he tried. Who could feel invincible with feet and a back that felt so damn sore after standing for a solid hour and a half?

Stacy nudged him. "You okay?"

He nodded, forced a smile. "Yep."

She pursed her lips, looking doubtful. "You sure?"

Another nod. "I'm sure."

He wasn't, but he was determined not to let it show until after they were out of here, maybe not even then. Another thing feeding into the glumness of his thoughts was, of course, the prospect of the looming confrontation with Janine. If he'd responded to her text earlier or dealt with the situation in a forthright way, maybe things wouldn't have been so bad. There would've been anger and hurt feelings regardless but deliberately ignoring her to the point of turning his phone off for the duration of the show took things to a much graver place. The damage might well be irreparable. That wasn't necessarily a given, though. The real crux of the matter was whether he cared enough to fight for his marriage and somehow atone for his deceit.

He didn't know the answer to that yet.

Craig shook his head.

What a fucking thing, to feel so good and so bad at the same time.

Another nudge from Stacy took him out of this spiraling line of thought. When she was sure she had his attention, she took a pointed look around at the place. "Look at us, man. The last ones standing."

Though a few patrons remained in the bar area, the three of them were the last of the standing spectators in front of the stage. At first Craig assumed she was referring to this fact alone, but something in her tone suggested otherwise.

Their old friend group from back in the day had been more than just the three of them. There'd been other core members, tight friends, not just people from the periphery who floated in and out of their orbit. People Craig had loved just as much as Stacy and Bill. As he craned his head around, he could imagine where those others would be standing if they were here tonight. How they'd look, the clothes they'd be wearing, what they'd be drinking. The images were so vivid, so seemingly three-dimensional, a shiver went through his body.

The three of them actually here tonight were just what remained of that group, the ones who hadn't faded all the way out of each other's lives, either by death or estrangement or great geographical distance.

Oddly, the absent friend he saw most clearly was Jarrett, the one who'd been gone the longest. He imagined Jarett standing right in front of him now, engaged with them in deep, passionate conversation about the show. Of all of them, it was Jarrett who'd been the most devoted to music, the truest believer in the spiritual power of rock and roll, and the one who'd most doggedly chased a place for himself in the world of rock before giving up after realizing his window of opportunity had come and gone. Rock was a young man's game, at least at the aspirational level, and he'd gotten too old to have any realistic hope of breaking in.

Craig could really almost see the guy, decked out in his old trench coat, a pair of black shades hooked over the collar of his Hanoi Rocks t-shirt, Sid Vicious-style dog collar and padlock around his neck, mass of blond hair Aqua Net-ted into the stratosphere, smirking over the rim of a Heineken as he yammered on about the show in his California surfer-like voice. Never mind that he'd never surfed or been to California at all.

Fucking Jarrett.

Maybe the biggest Bile Lords fan there ever was.

Twelve years dead now after hanging himself, frozen forever in time in the minds of those who'd known him. Unable to ever move on or find some other way of filling the holes in his life.

Craig missed all the ones who were gone, but he missed Jarrett most of all.

"I think I need a drink. You guys want anything? Maybe join me at the bar?" He glanced in that direction. "There's more than enough room now."

Bill shook his head. "I'm good. Hit my limit for the night. Maybe went a little past it. Probably gonna feel like shit tomorrow."

Stacy said, "I'm gonna wait right here, in case Rodney actually turns up and delivers on his promise instead of blowing us off. You can bring me a High Life, though."

At the bar, Craig ordered the High Life Stacy had requested and a tall can of PBR for himself. Something less potent than another double IPA felt wise. Still in relative possession of his faculties, he wanted to lessen his chances of doing something stupid, like, say, calling Janine and blathering a load of combative nonsense while slurring his words like a buffoon.

By the time he returned to where his friends were standing, Rodney had emerged from wherever he'd been lurking throughout the show. The old roadie acknowledged him with a nod and a verbal greeting that to Craig felt overly familiar, given he'd still only just met the guy and had conversed with him in only the most minimal way. Thinking about this made him frown, because it raised questions about why this guy had insinuated himself in their midst in the first place. Why them and not some other group of oldsters at the show?

Random chance, most likely, but Craig had no real idea, having been in the bathroom when the guy showed up.

Anyway, did it really matter?

Probably not.

Stacy snagged her new High Life from him and slugged some back. "You're just in time."

Craig popped open his PBR. "Oh, yeah? How so?"

She smiled, arching an eyebrow as she glanced at Rodney. "Because thanks to our new pal here we're about to hang out with the fucking Bile Lords on their tour bus."

Craig's brow knitted. "Huh."

Stacy flashed a disgruntled look. "Oh, fuck. I know that tone. That's your party pooper tone."

Craig sighed. "I just don't know what's the right thing to do. Maybe I should go home. Maybe there's still time to fix things."

Until the moment he uttered these words, his conscious line of thought on the subject of his endangered marriage was trending in the precise opposite direction, so hearing them come out of his mouth surprised him. He knew right away it was some fearful part of his subconscious surging to the forefront, reminding him of the painful realities he'd have to grapple with if he allowed things to slide toward a breakup scenario. There were so many questions he'd barely considered. Where would he live? What would his daughter think? Would she hate him, maybe even refuse to talk to him?

Fuck.

Once again, he felt on the verge of being overwhelmed.

The look on Stacy's face softened, her empathetic side showing itself again. "You have to do what you think is best. It's okay. But . . . Craig . . ." She smiled, shook her head, glanced around. "This chance ain't ever gonna come around again. You know?"

He nodded.

He did know.

And he still felt torn in too many uncertain directions, but sometimes in life acting on impulse was all you could do.

"Fuck it. Let's do it."

Rodney grinned, clapping him on the arm. "That's the spirit! Now, if you folks are decided, let's go meet ourselves a goddamn rock and roll star."

He led them toward an open door to the left of the stage, behind which Craig knew was the club's modest backstage area. It was a room he'd spent a bit of time in decades ago, when he and the rest of the gang had come out to see one of Jarrett's bands play a gig here. He couldn't remember which band that'd been, except that it'd been multiple decades ago, something he knew because it'd been one of Jarrett's projects where he was the centerpiece, the frontman. Long before he started aging in the scene, dropping down to side man status, playing bass instead of six-string or singing lead. Playing someone else's songs instead of his own.

They passed through the backstage area and through a back door into the rear parking lot behind the club. Rodney held the door open, nodding and smiling until everyone was out of the club. Then he closed the door and trailed after them at an unhurried pace, hanging back a bit as they continued into the center of the lot and spent some time gawking at the bus.

Craig estimated it was roughly the size of a Greyhound passenger bus, only a bit wider and with darkly tinted windows. It had a custom black wrap imprinted with the Bile Lords logo and an image of a much younger Kyle Bile's face. Stretching across the entire back edge of the lot, it was an imposing presence that loomed over the club.

"Wow."

Stacy, gazing up at the singer's image on the side of the vehicle, eyes goggling like those of an international tourist marveling over the ancient majesty of pyramids.

Craig, next to her, whispered, "It's just a bus."

She gave him a sneering look and took out her phone. "Right. Like the Empire State is just a building. Think of all the debauched shit that's taken place on that thing over the years. The stuff of legend."

"I'm pretty sure it's just a rental," Bill chimed in.

Stacy turned the sour look his way, only now it was even more withering. "Shut up, please. Let me have my illusions. They're all I've got anymore."

Rodney chuckled as he came forward, stepping between Stacy and Bill as the former raised her phone and snapped quick shots of the bus. "It's true we weren't traveling in this thing during the *Hollywood Babylon* days, but it has seen its fair share of decadence. Kyle might be a little older now, but he's still got the same, uh . . . *appetites* he always had." He took Stacy's hands in his own and held on to her as he added, "Before we board, do me a favor and put the phones away.

Kyle doesn't like them being out when he's in a private setting."

Stacy's face drooped. "I'm sorry. I don't want to make anyone mad. I just—"

Rodney patted her arm. "Oh, it ain't a problem out here. Take all the pictures you want, little lady. I'd just ask that you wait until maybe tomorrow before posting them anywhere. Like I said, Kyle's real protective of his privacy. He wouldn't want anyone else seeing them photos just yet and getting the idea they could come out and hang like you three."

Stacy's smile came back. "I get it. It's no problem."

She made a show of turning her phone off and stuffing it down in a pocket of her leather jacket.

Craig had no need of making any such gesture, his phone being already off and tucked away, but the way the old rock star's assistant kept emphasizing the man's desire for a strict level of privacy struck him as strange. This wasn't the 80s or the 90s anymore. Hell, it wasn't even 2015, which was maybe the last time the mainstream press would have given a shit about any misbehavior on the part of Kyle Bile.

Hell, looked at from another angle, it could be argued that any form of unlikely controversy that might arise from images or videos recorded by their phones would be a good thing for the Bile Lords. The old "any press is good press" adage.

But, whatever.

This was important to Stacy, and he wasn't about to taint the experience for her with any further snarky comments or questions. He did wonder whether she had taken any offense at being referred to as "little lady", because it was the kind of disrespectful and sneakily misogynistic remark he'd known her to react negatively to in the past, but she gave no outward indication of it. A little part of him wanted to speak up on her behalf, but he had a hunch that type of white knight interjection would come across as equally disrespectful. If the chance to have a private audience with an idol and decades-long crush was more important to her than putting some condescending asshole in his place, so be it.

The pneumatic two-panel doors of the bus already stood open as they arrived, the stairs beyond awaiting their ascent. Rodney stood off to the side, one scrawny arm braced against the edge of the doorframe as he nodded at them to step on up.

Stacy was the first to start up the steps.

Then Bill.

Craig went up last, but only after a final hesitant glance at the old roadie. Something in the man's gaze changed in the subtlest way when their eyes met, a little shift or flicker he was sure hadn't been there as his friends filed by him. He got the sense Rodney knew he didn't find his gruff old rogue persona as ingratiating as they did. Maybe that was an error in perception, his imagination seeing something that wasn't there. Wouldn't be the first time.

He didn't think so, though.

At the top of the steps, they bypassed the empty driver's seat and filed through an arched opening into a large lounge outfitted with restaurant-style booths along one side and a long, plush leather couch along the other side. Beyond this area was a kitchenette with cabinets, a sink, bar, microwave, and refrigerator. In the lounge, a large flatscreen television was bracketed to the wall above the booths, while another, slightly smaller one was mounted above the bar in the kitchenette. Past the kitchenette was a door with a curtain drawn across it. Craig assumed Kyle and the other members of his band were somewhere on the other side of that, because there was no sign of them out here in the main compartment.

Everything looked shiny and new, state-of-the-art, or at least so well-cared-for the difference between new and slightly-less-new was impossible to discern. Stacy and Bill made noises of appreciation, repeatedly remarking on how "nice" everything looked.

Craig couldn't disagree.

The inside of the bus was certainly the furthest thing from the grungy rolling pit he'd envisioned prior to leaving the club, if only because the modern-day edition of the Bile Lords hadn't struck him as an act that could afford such relatively luxurious traveling accommodations. The band had sold millions of albums once upon a time. Long ago. Craig supposed it was possible Kyle still had a chunk of the fortune he'd earned back then, enough to prioritize comfort when he took his reconfigured new version of the band out on the road. Probably also saved some money by paying his hired nobodies very little compared to what it'd take to tour with the classic lineup. All uninformed supposition on Craig's part, of course, but he had a feeling it wasn't too far off the mark.

At Rodney's invitation, they sat, with Stacy and Craig situating themselves on opposite sides of a tabletop bracketed to the wall while Bill plopped down on the opposing sofa.

"You folks make yourselves comfortable while I check in with the boss man. There's beer in the fridge and harder stuff under the bar. Help yourselves. I doubt we'll keep you waiting long."

And with that, he left them alone, striding into the kitchenette and disappearing into the rear compartment. Craig caught a momentary glimpse of bunk beds and another area past that as he twitched the curtain aside. Through an open door farther back, he saw a corner of a larger bed, but all these things fell from view as the curtain was tugged back into place from the other side.

Stacy downed the remainder of her latest High Life and carried the empty bottle into the kitchenette, where she dumped it in a trash receptacle she found under the bar. Pulling open the refrigerator, she stepped back and gaped at the contents with exaggerated astonishment.

She glanced back at Craig, grinning. "Holy shit, dude. This thing is packed with enough brewskis to keep a frat party going most of the fucking night. Bunch of that snobby shit you like, too."

There was a rattle of bottles as she reached inside and shuffled some of the selection around before emerging with a bottle of Heineken. She popped the cap off with an opener attached to the wall and came back into the lounge, plopping back into the same seat.

Craig raised an eyebrow. "Heineken? Not exactly your usual."

She shrugged before taking a deep slug from the bottle. "Nope, but it just kind of feels right." The way she looked at him clued him in on what she meant. "Can you imagine how jazzed he'd be by all this?"

By "he" she of course meant their forever absent old friend.

Craig nodded. "Yeah."

Maybe she was right. The version of Jarrett they'd all known from the good old days would absolutely have been thrilled to find himself in this setting, having spent much of his life dreaming about being out on a real rock and roll tour. He chose not to voice his guess about how the older, disillusioned version of the same guy might react to this situation, how temporary exposure to a slice of everything he'd ever wanted would feel like a taunt.

He was still thinking about that when the hot girl from the merch table flicked an edge of the curtain aside and emerged into the kitchenette, not looking at them as she went straight to the fridge and took out a bottle of Stella Artois, throwing the door shut again with a lot more force than seemed necessary, rattling the other bottles inside.

She popped the cap off with the same wall opener Stacy had used, ignoring the cap as it clattered to the floor. She took out her phone and swiped at the screen as she leaned her shapely ass against the edge of the counter in the kitchenette. Though she hadn't said anything, everything about her demeanor made it clear she was not happy about something. Whether that something had to do with them or an unrelated matter was unclear.

The three of them exchanged slightly uneasy looks.

Of course, it was Stacy who spoke up.

She'd never had much tolerance for uneasy silences. To understate.

"Something wrong, dear?"

The merch girl didn't look away from her phone, saying nothing for a drawn-out moment, barely even seeming to breathe until a put-upon sigh emerged from her lips. "You could say that."

It was one of the frostiest utterances Craig had ever heard from anyone. The impression that she might be less than thrilled about the presence of he and his friends deepened. Once again, looks were exchanged among them, though this time Stacy rolled her eyes.

Hoping he might head off the snide remarks he was sure Stacy yearned to unleash at the girl, Craig stood up and wobbled into the kitchenette, all the alcohol he'd imbibed having more of a lingering effect than anticipated. It was true he'd sobered some during the show but not entirely, it seemed.

The merch girl looked up as he came within several feet of her vicinity, a corner of her mouth ticking up in a look of distaste. He made direct eye contact with her for a fraction of a second, looking away immediately because the only other option was to stop and stare in the creepiest way possible. Up close, she was even more beautiful than he'd thought. Even as he looked away, the image of that gorgeous face was seared indelibly into his mind. A little ache flared in his chest as he was briefly overcome with the fervent desire to be thirty years younger. At the same time, he was grateful to have had the presence of mind to look away instead of becoming hopelessly transfixed, which would have been mortifying.

After tossing down the remainder of his PBR, he crumpled the can and disposed of it in the same receptacle Stacy had used.

Then he opened the fridge.

His mouth dropped open.

Stacy had not exaggerated.

This wasn't some hotel mini-fridge. It was a full-sized unit, and except for a handful of spots where bottles had been removed, every inch of space was filled with beers. All the shelves, all the side compartments, every food tray. It was enough beer to make Homer Simpson weep with joy.

He picked out a random craft IPA, one he'd never heard of, opened it, and returned to his seat.

Glancing at Stacy after taking a sip, he said, "You were right."

"I always am."

She looked again at the sullen merch girl, speaking before Craig could think of some other way of heading off whatever type of provocation she had in mind. "What's your name, sweetie?"

Craig almost spit out his next sip of beer.

Sweetie. Good lord.

The girl didn't look away from her phone and did not immediately respond, but a touch of color bloomed in her otherwise pale cheeks. She looked like she might be gripping her phone a little harder, too. Being called "sweetie", whether as an innocent term of endearment or a subtle dig, was clearly not something she appreciated. Despite her beauty, she projected a hard-edged outer persona, an invisible shell that might as well have come with a sign that said *do not engage* or *keep your distance*. Or both.

Like some dangerous animal in a zoo enclosure.

Or it might all be a pose, a means of protecting herself in the rough and tumble environment of a traveling rock band. In the company of people she knew and trusted, she might be all softness and vulnerability.

Regardless, antagonizing her probably wasn't the best idea, unless the goal was to get kicked off the bus. He reached across the narrow table space and touched Stacy's arm, giving her a look he hoped might silently communicate this concern. She responded with another roll of her eyes, but she refrained from further attempts at provoking the standoffish merch girl.

The girl stayed where she was perhaps another full minute before she tucked her phone in a back pocket and disappeared through the curtain into the back.

Craig sighed in relief. "Maybe leave that one alone if she comes out again."

Bill chuckled. "Yeah, she really doesn't seem all that sociable."

Stacy sneered, gulped beer. "Fuck that bitch. I don't like anyone taking attitude with me. Especially young people. What was she, twenty, at most?"

Bill nodded. "Looked about that, yeah."

Stacy snorted. "She could be my granddaughter. Also, it bugged me a little, the phone thing. We're not allowed to have ours out, but she gets to play with hers in front of us? Felt like she was rubbing our noses in it."

Craig shrugged. "I get it, but you don't know what kind of sway she has with this group, what the dynamics are. She's on the inside, part of the family, we're outsiders. Strangers. You piss her off enough, maybe you don't get to meet Kyle."

Stacy groaned, the look on her face still imbued with a tinge of defiance as she shook her head, but she said nothing further on the subject.

They'd spoken in hushed tones, with frequent cautious glances toward the curtain over the door at the back of the kitchenette. Being in this strange setting, just the three of them for the time being in a state of nervous anticipation, they were not unlike a group of onlookers along a parade route awaiting a glimpse of some important personage. Only what they were actually waiting for was a sign that a rock legend would deign to meet them. Craig didn't think he'd be fully convinced on that count until the man was out here in the lounge with them.

As it turned out, they didn't have much longer to wait, because moments later the curtain was swept roughly aside and a procession of four individuals filed out of the rear compartment into the kitchenette. Rodney was first through the door. He acknowledged Craig and his friends with a nod. A tall, skinny man Craig recognized as the young lead guitarist was next. Wearing mirrored sunglasses and clutching a pack of smokes, he strode rapidly through the lounge without glancing at the guests, the heavy trod of his boots loud on the floor. A moment later, they heard him descending the steps out of the bus.

Kyle and the merch girl were next through the door. The girl glared at them from the kitchenette while Kyle veered toward the refrigerator. He opened it with far too much force, causing a stubby brown bottle of Red Stripe to topple out and break on the floor.

"*Goddamnmotherfuckinsonofawhore.*"

The slurred way he ran it all together made the profane outburst sound like one word. He reached into the fridge, snagged a bottle of

Beck's, and threw the door shut again, rounding on the girl and jabbing an index finger in her face. "Clean that shit up, bitch."

Only *bitch* sounded more like *bish*.

Craig and Stacy shared an apprehensive look.

The girl knocked his hand away. "Fuck you, Kyle. Make Rodney do it."

Kyle glared at her.

Then he snorted laughter. "You heard her, Rods."

Rodney's ever-present smile never slipped. "You got it, boss."

After opening his bottle, the rock singer came forward into the lounge while Rodney again retreated into the back, presumably in search of cleanup materials. Kyle looked like a man on the listing deck of a ship, struggling to stay upright as high winds and waves lashed the vessel. His eyes were glassy and his mass of dyed-black hair was a tangled mess. Close up, the dye job was revealed as flawed or in need of touching up, with grey visible in random spots as well as at the roots.

He'd changed out of his leather stage clothes, donning socks, a loose-fitting pair of grey sweatpants, and nothing else. In the absence of the tight leather vest he'd worn for the show, it was even more obvious how out-of-shape he'd become, his thick chest hair only slightly obscuring the size of his man-boobs. His socks were wet with beer from the bottle he'd broken, a thing he gave no indication of noticing.

Kyle plopped down on the sofa a few feet from where Bill sat, propped one leg over the other, and leaned back. He draped an arm over the back of the sofa and took a swig of Beck's. Then he took a squinting look around at his guests, appearing mildly confused about who they were and why they were on the bus. "You're the ones Rodney was talking about. The . . . fans."

Stacy nodded. "That's right. Fans all the way back to the *Hollywood Babylon* days. Saw you on tour a bunch of times, all of us, from the early shows opening for Whitesnake to when you were headlining arenas and stadiums. You're part of the soundtrack of our lives." She gave an embarrassed little laugh that was unlike her. "Same story you've heard a million times, I'm sure."

A blearily thoughtful look dawned on Kyle's face. He opened his mouth to say something before abruptly breaking into a brief but violent coughing fit. Heaving himself toward the edge of the couch, he leaned forward and thumped his chest with a fist.

Then he fell back and heaved a big, ragged breath, the fit seeming to have passed. He took a smaller swig of beer and grunted soft laughter. "I miss the arenas. The big crowds. Being young and on top of the world." He looked around at each of them again. "Look at you fuckers. Old as shit like me. Ain't it a bitch."

Once again, it was Stacy who spoke for them. "You got that right, but you know what? The size of the crowds might not be the same, but you put on a hell of a show tonight. We were all blown away." She glanced at her friends. "Isn't that right, fellas?"

Craig nodded. "Oh, absolutely." He indicated Bill with a tilt of his head. "And I'll be honest, until our friend there saw a flyer for the show last week, none of us even knew the Bile Lords were still around. I didn't know what to expect tonight, but you kicked a lot of ass."

Bill grunted in agreement. "Metric tons of ass."

Kyle looked at Bill, brow knitting in apparent confusion. Then he said, "Why aren't you drinking?"

Bill shifted around a little on the couch. "Well, you know . . . I had some beers earlier, but—"

"Fuck that," the singer said, cutting him off. "Whatever goddamn excuse you were about to make. Fuck all that shit. You need a beer. This is a strictly no sober people allowed party." He looked toward the kitchen, where his assistant was about done cleaning up the mess his boss had made. "Yo, Rod-meister. Bring this man a beer."

From the look on his face, Bill clearly wasn't thrilled about the idea, but he didn't say anything. Craig understood. The man who'd sung some of the most enduring rock anthems of the late 80s insisting on you having a beer with him wasn't the kind of thing that happened every day. It was one of those situations where saying no just wasn't a real option.

Rodney had dumped the broken bottle pieces in the trash and was soaking up the beer with a mop. "On it. One second."

He stowed the mop in a bucket, leaned the mop handle against a wall, and snagged another bottle from the fridge, showing it to Bill. "Will a Corona do?"

Bill shrugged, fully giving in now. "Sure."

Rodney popped the cap off and brought him the bottle. Bill accepted it with a nod of reluctant appreciation and took a token sip. With that done, Rodney returned to the kitchenette, grabbed the mop and bucket, and disappeared through the curtain into the back.

Kyle turned his attention to the sullen merch girl, who'd been standing silent several feet away, right at the edge of the kitchenette. "Over here, baby doll," he said, patting a thigh.

She hesitated only a moment before coming to him with a slinky sway of her hips and a seductive pout, curling into his lap and resting a head on his shoulder, then sliding her fingers into the thick mat of his chest hair. The sneering look of defiance on her face told them she didn't give a shit what any of them thought about the brazen display of intimacy with a man so much older than she was, daring them to say anything against it. The sneer became especially pronounced when she directed it at Stacy.

Then, sensing she'd at least mildly scandalized them, the sneer soon gave way to a pleased smile.

Kyle appeared oblivious to the tense dynamic between his girl and his guests.

He took a swig of Beck's and said, "Gotta apologize for the lack of rock and roll glamor. Thirty-five years ago, we were on private planes instead of a goddamn bus. I'd have supermodels in lingerie lounging all over the place, rock press vampires clamoring to talk to me, loads of kiss-ass sycophants and scenesters hanging around trying to look cooler-than-thou, maybe luck into appearing in the background of pictures that end up in *Rolling Stone* or whatever, but . . ." He tiredly craned his head around, emphasizing the absence of all those things. "I didn't get to stay cool for generations like the Stones thanks to grunge. There ain't no glamor anymore. Andy Warhol has left the fucking building."

Craig had the impression he'd given versions of this speech on numerous occasions, a guess based in part on the way all that wordage spewed out with greater coherence than he'd seemed capable of in his current condition.

At the same time, the man's words struck him as nothing but the plain truth. This was the rock star divested of artifice and pretense, the damaged and time-degraded human being behind the image crafted long ago, one he wore like a frayed old suit destined for the donation bin, stripped of his past glories and painfully aware of it, if not exactly at peace with it.

The merch girl squirmed in his lap and sat up straighter, appearing to take umbrage with what he'd said. "Don't talk like that. You're Kyle fucking Bile, goddammit, rock and roll legend and sexy-ass motherfucker. The world just needs to be reminded again. That's why we're doing all this. Remember?"

Kyle breathed another tired sigh before giving a reluctant nod. "I know, baby. I'm just wiped out from the show, that's all. You know how I get emotional after sometimes."

The girl put her head back on his shoulder, apparently mollified. "I know. Just please don't say those things again."

Her voice sounded smaller than before, softer and less certain, with maybe a bit of underlying fear, as if she were trying hard to convince herself the things she was saying were true and not just some desperate fantasy. Hearing that, it became possible to feel sympathy for the real person beneath the hard-edged exterior. This was a young girl who'd clearly bought into all the most appealing parts of the rock and roll myth, but who'd missed out on the glory days by decades. Unfortunately, in chasing that dream, she'd hitched her wagon to a guy far removed from any appropriate age range for her who was, from all appearances, a hopeless late-stage alcoholic with a capacity for emotional abuse at the very least.

Craig and Stacy exchanged another look, and once again Craig knew they were thinking the same thing. Maybe it was time to cut this short and say their goodbyes. They'd done what they'd come here to do and it'd probably be best to leave before a messy situation turned even more uncomfortable.

Then, right as Craig was about to get to his feet and begin making their excuses, Kyle looked right at him and said, "Maybe the three of you could tell me something. You're all from around here, right? This Drayton Falls place?"

"Uh . . ." Though hesitant to commit himself to another line of conversation that might delay their exit by several minutes at least, Craig couldn't quite bring himself to blow off the question. He nodded. "Yes. We all are. Why do you ask?"

Kyle smiled. "Well, let's just say I've heard some . . . *interesting* stories about this area."

Craig strove to keep his face blank. "What kind of stories?"

As if he didn't already know. It'd been a while since the last time, but on occasion throughout his life, he'd come into contact with other people from away who'd made similar inquiries. Always about the same thing.

The singer chuckled. "Come on, man. I get the feeling you already know. Is Drayton Falls really a cursed town, a place where strange things have a habit of happening?"

The three locals exchanged wary glances, something both the singer and his girlfriend took obvious note of, their gazes keener and more intensely interested than Craig would have thought possible prior to this conversational detour. He had a feeling this wasn't a random topic, that Kyle had some as-yet-unrevealed reason for bringing it up.

He shrugged. "Some people do say that, I suppose. Mostly superstitious old-timers." He thought about what he'd said and added, "*Real* old-timers, I mean, folks who still remember when Eisenhower was president."

This was not the absolute truth. As a man in his late fifties who'd lived in the town since birth, he was well aware of its reputation. Though he'd had no direct experience with some of the more outlandish types of paranormal or otherworldly phenomena reputed to happen in the area, he'd stood in places where he believed he'd heard the whispering voices of the dead, in old houses and cemeteries, even in some of the wooded areas he and his friends had explored when they were young. But he'd heard stories of scarier things from people who had his unequivocal trust. And not just from shriveled-up nonagenarians.

People his age and younger.

Much younger, sometimes.

The bottom line was he knew for a fact strangeness of likely supernatural origin was a real thing. As for why he sought to downplay the notion, it was the ingrained instinct of most Drayton Falls natives to be evasive on the subject when talking to outsiders. Each generation had this lesson instilled almost at birth and then reinforced throughout childhood until it took hold. Drayton Falls coexisted with the outside world in many ways, but it mostly kept its mysteries to itself.

Kyle stared evenly at him for several moments, then looked at Stacy. "What do you say, sweet thing? Is it like he says? Just a bunch of superstition?"

Stacy's expression was guarded. "Yeah, pretty much. It's just . . . you know . . . campfire tales."

Kyle grunted, turned his head to look at Bill. "What do you say, baldie? Same bullshit?"

Bill's only answer was a shrug.

Kyle tossed his head back and unleashed a loud groan of annoyance, followed by a sneering look of disdain he leveled first at Craig and then at Stacy. "Look, I'm just gonna come out and say it. I know you're feeding me a line of shit. And the reason I know that is you guys aren't just here by random chance tonight. You were chosen."

Craig was so taken aback by this statement he was at first at a loss as to how to respond. His mouth opened as his face twisted with confusion, but no words emerged. Then he glanced at Stacy, who appeared just as flabbergasted.

Kyle laughed.

His girlfriend did, too, smiling in a real, unguarded way for the first time in their presence.

The singer gave her a nudge. "Go get the letters, babe. Time to lay our cards on the table." He directed a wink at Stacy. "Most of them, least ways."

Stacy looked at Craig, mouthing the question: *Letters?*

Craig shrugged.

He had no idea what the man was talking about, but he did know he didn't much care for the singer's stark shift in demeanor. Maybe it was just paranoia, but it seemed to Craig his latest utterances contained a hint of malice.

Maybe more than just a hint.

Craig rose to his feet with an abruptness that surprised even him, indicating to Stacy with a tilt of his head that she should get up, too.

She was on her feet in an instant, clearly as unnerved as Craig.

Craig said, "No idea what any of this is about, but we're leaving."

Just as he was turning toward the front of the bus, the merch girl launched herself off Kyle's lap and slammed her palms against Stacy's chest, eliciting a cry of pain and surprise as she knocked the older woman back into her seat. Craig's heart lurched painfully in his chest in reaction to the unexpected burst of violence. He wanted to intervene, but the pain and his galloping heart scared him, made him afraid to move at all. For about the millionth time in recent history, he cursed his age and deteriorating physical condition. Another stab of pain knifed through him as he watched the merch girl repel a second attempt by Stacy to get to her feet, slapping her hard multiple times across the face, forehand and backhand blows.

Stacy sobbed.

The merch girl jabbed a finger in her face. "Stay down, bitch, or you'll get worse than that."

She cracked her palm across Stacy's face yet again for emphasis.

Then she stalked out of the lounge and disappeared into the rear compartment.

The sight of Stacy's tears and quaking shoulders filled Craig's heart with another kind of pain. It hurt him to the core of his being to see the love of his life in such terrified distress. Because, yes, underneath it all, that's what she was to him. His own stupidity many years ago had permanently altered the trajectory of both their lives, but that didn't change the truth. More than anything, he wanted to go to her and offer comfort, take her out of here, but she looked like he did, stunned and afraid to move.

Craig looked toward the front of the bus upon hearing footsteps from that direction. The lanky guitar player had come back inside, but now he had a gun and it was aimed at Craig's chest, a development that did nothing to calm his nerves or racing heart. The young man's eyes were inscrutable behind his mirrored shades and his slack expression revealed nothing, but he appeared relaxed, holding the gun loosely, most of his weight shifted to one side in a lazy stance, the opposite of what Craig would expect of a person who truly believed he might actually have to pull a trigger. As if the mere threat of the gun would suffice to keep everyone in line. Did the guitarist's bored posture suggest a lack of genuine deadly intent?

Maybe so.

Regardless, it'd be foolish not to take the threat the gun represented seriously. The revolver's chambers were filled with bullets, and the barrel was still pointed at his chest with the guitarist's forefinger inside the trigger guard. All it'd take to end his life was one careless twitch of that finger.

The look on Kyle's face hardened. "Just sit back down a while, man. Christ, you should see your face. It's red as a beet. We've got business together, all of us, so try calming yourself while we see it through."

Much as Craig hated to admit it, this was good advice. He took in a deep breath and slowly let it out, then he gently lowered himself back into his seat, holding a hand hard to his chest as he willed his heart to settle back into a normal rhythm. Not helping matters was how strange and deliriously disorienting these new developments were. An impromptu meet-and-greet with an aging rock star turned hostage situation—or perhaps something even worse—was so out there it was almost impossible to comprehend as being real.

A spark of anger flared inside him as he met Kyle's smirking gaze. "This what you do now that your career's in the toilet? Terrorize and rob old fans?"

Kyle shook his head. "It's nothing as mundane as that. You'll see for yourself soon enough."

As if on cue, the merch girl came out of the rear compartment. Clutched in one hand she had a stack of crumpled old envelopes, all bound together with a rubber band. It was clear the envelopes had all taken a journey through the US mail at some point in the distant past. They were all ragged at the top where they'd been cut open, and Craig glimpsed fading postmarks and peeling stamps. Then he perceived something else he first chalked up to a trick of his imagination, but the thought lingered, intensifying as he watched the merch girl hand the stack of letters to her boyfriend.

Was there something . . . *familiar* about the piece of handwriting he'd glimpsed on the top envelope?

No. It can't be. That's crazy.

But as Kyle removed the rubber band and began sorting through the letters, mere suspicion began the journey toward stunned certainty.

Stacy wiped tears away and sat forward in her seat. "Wait. Is that . . ."

Kyle flashed a grin her way. "Yes, you're starting to get it now, both of you. I see it in your eyes." He withdrew a single letter from the stack and set the others on the couch next to him. "So here's another question for you. No point lying this time, because I already know the answer. Did you assholes once upon a time have a close friend named Jarrett?"

Stacy sniffled. "He sent you fan letters."

Still grinning, Kyle nodded. "You got it, sweet thing. You know, you don't look half bad for an old hag. I would've banged the shit out of you back in the day."

Stacy's face crinkled in disgust. "Go to hell."

The merch girl smacked the back of her head. "Shut the fuck up."

Kyle laughed. "Oh, the matter of my afterlife destination was settled a long time ago. I'm definitely going to hell, but I'm gonna do everything I can to delay my arrival there. Matter of fact, that's part of what this is all about. You see, when I was a young man, I did about the most cliched Satanic Panic era thing an 80s rock and roller could do. I made a deal with Ol' Scratch himself. The usual terms. Sell your soul for wealth and fame and all that shit. You know how the story goes. Worked out great for a while."

Craig snorted.

The pain in his chest had subsided, his heartbeat having resumed something resembling a normal rate. At the same time, that spark of anger was on the verge of turning into a flame. "Not that I believe any of that nonsense, but what's it got to do with us? Or with Jarrett?"

Kyle scowled. "I'm getting to that, you impatient motherfucker." He withdrew the letter he'd selected from its envelope, revealing crinkly sheets of paper torn from a spiral notebook. The pages were yellow at the edges and smeared with ink from the cheap pens that'd been used to write the missives. "As you can see, your dead friend sent me a bunch of letters. Not to our old fan club, mind you, but to me, care of the record company. I got loads of letters when the band was riding high. Most of them I never saw. We had people that went through them for us. If they included a return envelope, they'd get back a signed photo, maybe some stickers or patches. Sometimes, just every once in a while, there'd be letters that stood out from the pack enough to get forwarded to me. Some of it was what you'd think. Lipstick-kissed letters from hot chicks who sent nudie photos or used panties. Phone numbers, too. I'd have the really special ones flown out and put up at a nice hotel long enough to fuck them before sending their asses back to Peoria or wherever-the-fuck."

He said these things in a wistful tone, smiling all the while, but now the smile faded, his expression becoming more serious. "Jarrett's letters stood out in a different way. Not to speak ill of the dead, but it's fair to say the guy may have been a wee bit . . . *obsessed* with me. Like, he literally thought I was talking directly to him through my lyrics. Coded mental telegrams. Crazy, huh?"

Never in his life had Craig wanted to punch a person as much as he longed to ram a fist straight down Kyle Bile's throat right there and then. If he didn't think making the attempt might actually kill him, he might well have tried.

Stacy said, "Jarrett was a troubled soul, but we loved him."

Kyle's smile squirmed with smugness as he nodded and looked again at the sheaf of smudged and yellowed pages. "It's interesting you say that, because he talked about all of you in these letters, and a lot of what he had to say wasn't flattering." He looked up from the pages, smirking as he picked up the other letters in the stack and tossed them onto the little table space between Craig and Stacy. "Maybe you'd like to take a look for yourselves."

No longer held together with the rubber band, the stacked letters spread apart, a few dropping to the floor as they spilled over the edge. Craig's gaze roved over the crumpled old envelopes, heart thumping harder again at the closer view of his dead friend's handwriting. Any lingering doubt that it was actually Jarrett's was erased in an instant. It didn't matter that he hadn't seen his handwriting in years. His penmanship was distinctive, and he knew it as well as he knew the handwriting styles of his wife and daughter or either of his long-deceased parents.

Craig looked at the smirking singer. "I don't need to read them to guess what he had to say about me. Stacy's right. We loved him, and he loved us, something I know for a fact. But I also know we didn't always see eye-to-eye on things, and sometimes he probably thought he hated us. No matter what, though, the love was always there, under the surface. So I don't know what you think you're accomplishing by opening those old wounds, but you can go fuck yourself, you has-been pile of fucking garbage."

Stacy laughed. "Amen. Your new song sucks, by the way."

The merch girl yanked her hair, making her yelp.

Stacy surged to her feet and punched the girl dead-center in the face, knocking her straight down to the floor as blood erupted from her nose. The girl screeched in rage and pain, but Kyle and the gun-wielding guitarist had a different reaction, which was to roar with laughter.

The curtain in back was swept aside as the chubbier of the two roadies that had worked the stage earlier poked his head out and said, "Everything all right out here?"

Kyle was still laughing hard, but he waved a flailing hand in the roadie's direction, a gesture apparently meant to say, "Go on, get out of here," because the man immediately disappeared back into the rear compartment, drawing the curtain back over the opening.

The merch girl rose to her haunches and remained there a few moments with blood still dripping from her nose, glaring first at Kyle then at Stacy and back again, saving the worst of her fury for the singer. "She hurt me and you're *laughing?*"

The singer's immediate response was more laughter, but he soon managed to compose himself, perhaps sobered a bit by the murderous look on the girl's face. "Baby, I'm sorry, that was just so fucking wild, a little old lady knocking my badass girlfriend right the fuck out. I just . . ."

He laughed again, wiped spittle from his mouth.

The merch girl got to her feet. "She didn't knock me *out*. I didn't lose *consciousness*, you fucking asshole."

Her defiant tone vibrated with the promise of aggression. Hearing it made Craig want to call out a warning, but there wasn't time as the girl turned and moved fast, drilling a fist into Stacy's abdomen hard enough to bend her at the waist, air exploding from her lungs. Then she swung her fist a second time, connecting with Stacy's jaw and knocking her to the floor.

The merch girl loomed over Stacy, raising a foot as if she meant to drill the heel of her boot into the back of the older woman's head.

Craig made as if he meant to get up and intercede, but the guitarist placed the gun against the side of his head.

"Don't."

Kyle loudly cleared his throat, his next words laced with a cold tone devoid of the wild humor of moments ago. "Don't do that, bitch. You've made your fucking point, okay? I'm not done with them yet, you know that."

The girl held her foot poised over Stacy's head a moment longer before carefully returning it to the floor. "You laugh at me in that mean way again, it might be the last time you laugh at anything. Get me?"

She and the singer looked into each other's eyes for a tense moment, the only sound was that of Stacy sobbing on the floor.

Then Kyle nodded, tone more subdued as he said, "I get you. I apologize for the disrespect. Now, please, let's get back to business. Get that hag off the floor and back into her seat."

The girl sneered. "With pleasure."

She seized Stacy under the arms and hauled her off the floor, flinging her back into the seat with excessive force, making her cry out again before transitioning to a low and steady moan of discomfort.

Craig again wanted to go to her, but the gun pressed to his head kept him where he was. He glanced at Bill, who hadn't moved or said a word in the last several minutes. Something about his oddly dispassionate expression sent a deeper shiver of dread rippling through Craig's already trembling body.

Craig pressed a calming hand to his chest. "What's going on with you, man? You're giving off a strange fucking vibe."

Kyle chuckled.

Bill stared evenly back at Craig for a moment. Then he raised the Corona bottle to his mouth, took a sip, and looked away.

"Like I said, back to business." Kyle gestured at the guitarist, who took the gun away from Craig's head. "As I was saying before the chick fight broke out, your dead friend had a lot to say about all of you. He did say he loved you. I'll give you that. But he was bitter as hell. He said none of you really believed in him, that you thought his rock and roll dreams were unrealistic because he wasn't good enough to make it."

A brief but heavy silence ensued.

Craig and Stacy looked at each other. Stacy's eyes were red and watery, steadily leaking tears, but the look on her face was resolute. This was a time for truth, for telling things as they were instead of softening them with pretty lies as they had too often in the past.

Craig let out a weary breath. "He thought that because it was true. I never put it quite like that. So bluntly. Don't think any of us did. But he could tell. We were all supportive for a long time. If he says otherwise in these letters, it was a dirty lie. And you know what? He could tell a dirty lie now and then. We all could. None of us were angels. But we went to his shows. Saw all the mediocre bands he had over the years. Tried our best to hype him up because he was our friend and he was so fucking passionate about it. He loved music, loved rock and roll, and knew more about it than anyone I ever knew, but yeah, motherfucker, he wasn't good enough. And I think in the end he accepted that he was never gonna make it, and that's why he did what he did."

Kyle nodded thoughtfully.

Then he held up a finger, smiling. "Nice speech. I can tell you believe all that, and the thing is, you're not wrong. The poor bastard didn't just send me a mountain of letters over the years. I got tapes. Demos. His music. The best of it was competent but boring. The worst . . ." He shrugged. "Well, let's be kind, okay? In this one way, if no other. But you're wrong about why he died. He didn't kill himself because he thought he wasn't good enough."

He stopped there, letting what was yet unvoiced hang between them for a tense, gut-twisting moment.

Craig's hands clenched into fists.

Whatever he's about to say is a lie. It has to be. Remember that.

He swallowed and said, "Why did he do it, then?"

Kyle finished off his beer and held the empty longnecked bottle loosely between his fingers, letting it dangle. "He did it for me. As a sacrifice."

Craig just stared at him for a few seconds, stunned.

Then he snorted. "Bullshit."

Kyle was stone-faced as he gave his head a slow shake. "No, man. It's true, I swear." He lifted the one letter he'd taken out of its envelope, brandishing it like a trial lawyer displaying exhibit A. "The root of it is all right here. This is the letter where he first told me about your town. The strange things that happen. The literal creatures of the night. The dark magic that can be tapped into by those who know how. As someone who knows more than a little about these subjects, I was intrigued. He'd given me a number, just like all those hot-to-trot chicks hungry for my cock. I called him to learn more. Long story short, he eventually convinced me he was telling the truth." A small smile crept back onto his face. "So I told him some of my secrets. About the deal I'd made as a young man, the additional rituals and sacrifices I'd had to perform in later years just to keep the band alive, just to keep *myself* alive."

Craig looked at each of the faces arrayed around him. Stacy's showed only fear, anger, and an ever-deepening confusion. The merch girl's wide-eyed, avid look radiated sadistic delight and almost breathless anticipation. The guitarist still looked almost bored, but events had shown his physical cues were not to be trusted. The man's actual opinion on everything happening here remained a mystery.

The same was true of Bill, who'd taken to sipping his Corona more rapidly and still wouldn't look at him.

The one thing Craig sensed across the board was a distinct lack of skepticism, which was strange, because the things being suggested by the deranged singer were things a normal person would dismiss as absurd.

He sat up straighter, taking his hand away from his chest. "So . . . if I understand you correctly . . . what you're saying is . . . our friend ended his life, offered it to . . . *Satan* . . . to . . . what . . . benefit your fucking band?"

Kyle nodded. "Not just for me, mind you. For the sake of *his* all-time favorite band, which had crashed and burned. In 2014, I owed so much money it was insane. I was running around in a drug-mad haze, moving from place to place, hiding from collection agents, mob goons, and my other junkie friends. I was like Ray Liotta in *Goodfellas* toward the end, desperately spiraling. The standard blood rituals weren't working like they used to. Something drastic had to happen."

Craig's face twisted into a look of barely contained, seething hatred. "That 'something drastic' being this so-called sacrifice, which according to you was made of Jarrett's own free will."

Kyle made a sound of deepening annoyance. "Yes, goddammit. Didn't I just already fucking say so? Don't you see? A life freely offered jacks up the power of any occult ritual. I'd come to believe a Satanic ritual performed on the cursed ground of this godforsaken backwater would have even greater power. *Unparalleled* power. Jarrett also believed it would work. Which is why, at six in the evening on the sixth of June that year, Jarrett listened to his vinyl copy of *Hollywood Babylon* and invoked my name and the name of the band as he slipped the noose around his neck and kicked over the chair he'd climbed up on."

Once again, he fell silent, allowing his audience a chance to ponder his words.

When Craig looked at Stacy again, her tears had dried up. She was still afraid, just as he was, but anger was again surpassing fear. Beyond these surface emotions, he detected a sense of utter stupefaction, which mirrored his own reaction. He did not doubt Kyle believed everything he was saying. There'd been none of the normal tells he'd look for when someone was attempting to deceive him. Every word out of the man's mouth was the truth as he saw it, even if it sounded like absolute madness.

Craig longed to launch himself at him, claw his eyes out of his face, beat him without mercy until his flesh was pulped and bloody, every bone in his own hands broken from unleashing the full extent of his fury. It was galling to know that if he even tried such a thing his knees or his back—or both—would betray him before he could land a single feeble punch.

Instead of trying any of those things, he swallowed hard and spoke in the most even tone he could muster. "That's all very specific. Are you saying you were actually there in the room with him when he did it?"

Kyle smiled. "Yes. I bore witness to his sacrifice. Please understand, I didn't see it the same way you would, not as some final tragic waste, but rather as a selfless act of love."

"Love for you?" Stacy asked.

Kyle nodded. "Yes."

Craig said, "And what was the ultimate result of the sacrifice, from your point of view? Did it accomplish what you hoped for?"

Kyle's demeanor brightened the instant this question was asked.

"*Yes!*" He sat up straighter, a new eagerness in his voice. "Our latest single at the time took off like nothing we'd done since the 90s, shooting up multiple charts, gaining radio play across a broad spectrum of formats. It became an actual crossover hit. We started getting mainstream media coverage again, started playing arenas again, even selling out in some markets." He laughed, shaking his head in fond remembrance. "It was amazing, every glorious moment. So, yes, it worked, and yes, it was one-hundred fucking percent worth it. Jarrett's sacrifice allowed me to experience being back on top again, and I have no regrets."

Craig's hand shot out and snatched up the half-consumed bottle of IPA next to him on the tabletop, and he winged it at the singer with as much strength as he could summon. This all happened in one continuous motion, with no pause to adjust his grip on the bottle or lean forward to better gauge his aim. It was the only way he could do it without someone stepping in to stop him, and for one incredible, breathless moment, he was sure his aim would be true.

The distance between him and the singer wasn't significant. A direct hit would require only a small bit of luck. Unfortunately, at the last possible fraction of a second, Kyle flinched, jerking his head just far enough leftward for the bottle to sail by the side of his head by a margin of less than an inch, shattering against the window behind him. Startled instinct propelled him to the edge of the couch, pieces of broken glass tumbling off his shoulder to the upholstery.

The merch girl gasped and shouted, "Holy shit!"

The singer gaped at Craig in stunned disbelief before slowly turning his head to look at the wet window and the jagged fragments of the shattered bottle. Then, after an audible gulp as the nearness of his close call registered, he swiveled his head back around to again regard Craig in that same disbelieving way.

"You goddamn son of a bitch. You almost fucking brained me." He laughed, but there was a nervous edge to the sound that hadn't been there other times. "I'll be honest. I didn't think you had anything like that in you. Jesus." He gave his head a hard shake, appearing to recover somewhat from the shock of the incident. "Well, damn, you're not quite the impotent pussy I thought. I'd say you just made things worse for yourself, but what's the point? They can't get much worse than they're already about to get, so we might as well move on to the main event."

The merch girl let out a strange gasp of almost orgasmic-sounding laughter. "*Yes!* Finally."

Craig was shaking and still consumed with bitter disappointment. He'd known from the start a direct hit to the singer's face or forehead would not magically free them of this situation. They were outnumbered, for one thing, with more of Kyle's lackeys lurking in the rear compartment, and some of their adversaries had youth on their side. One of them had a gun. Worst of all, one of his friends maybe wasn't on his side, judging from Bill's continued squirrely behavior, the way he wouldn't say anything or look directly at him.

It was hopeless.

But it would have been so goddamn satisfying to see that bottle explode across the singer's face, the way he would have screamed from the pain of impact, the way blood would have flowed from glass slicing up his face. Inwardly, he cursed fate or God or Satan, whatever entity or quirk of bad luck had allowed Kyle to flinch at just the right moment to avoid that happening.

Kyle cupped his hands around his mouth and raised his voice, summoning all the considerable lung power of a veteran hard rock singer as he called out his next words: "*Yo, Rodney! Bring her on out here!*" He grinned and uttered his next words in a lower, more sinister tone, a rumbling near growl. "It's . . . showtime."

A moment later the old roadie pulled back the curtain at the back of the kitchenette and dragged a young girl out of the rear compartment. Craig recognized her right away. It was the same girl he'd noticed a couple of times earlier in the night. The one who'd seemed drunk or high to the point of imminent collapse each time he saw her, swaying to her own off-kilter beat as the heavy music roared and enveloped her in waves of unrelenting noise.

Attired in loose black pants and a grungy gray sweatshirt, she had the hollow-eyed, vacant look of a strung-out junkie, her face devoid of makeup and shiny with perspiration. Those other times, Craig had seen her from a distance. What he'd glimpsed then was concerning, but up close it was obvious this was a person in severe crisis. Skinny to the point of starvation, the clothes that would have been tight on a healthy person hung off her emaciated frame. Her black hair was disheveled and dirty. Bits of dried blood had collected along the edges of her fingernails, presumably from obsessively scratching at places on her body hidden by the drooping clothes. Shoulders hunched, she stared at the floor, unable or unwilling to make eye contact with anyone in the lounge.

The look on Stacy's face was a mix of repulsion and motherly concern, her fear once again melting away in the face of something that was, at least in the moment, more distressing than her own predicament. "Who is this girl and what have you done to her, you sick bastard?"

Kyle rose from the couch and approached the vacant-eyed girl. Instead of retreating or cringing away from him, she remained where she was as he draped an arm around her thin shoulders and drew her close. She slumped against him, pressing her head against his chest.

She whimpered a single word in a voice so low it was almost inaudible. "*Daddy*."

Kyle ruffled the girl's hair and kissed the top of her head. "I'm right here, baby," he said in a tone calculated to soothe. "And I'll be with you all the way to the end, I promise."

Craig's mind reeled as he struggled to make sense of what he was hearing. He looked at Stacy and saw she was equally astonished, mouth moving with no words emerging. Craig understood. It was hard to know what to say. Kyle's latest utterances unearthed new areas of confusion and dread.

He cleared his throat. "Hold on a goddamn minute. Are you saying what I think you're saying?"

Kyle smiled over the top of the girl's head. "In a few minutes, my daughter will surrender her life and soul to Satan so that the Bile Lords might rise to glory one more time."

Stacy's eyes were wide with horror. "You sick piece of shit. You can't do this."

Kyle's laughter exuded profound condescension. "Normies and their mundane ideas of morality never fail to amuse. Also, yes, I can. Who here would stop me?" More of that condescending laughter. "By the way, like Jarrett, Nona is offering this precious gift of her own free will."

Stacy snorted. "Bullshit. Bull-fucking-shit. I don't believe you."

Kyle shrugged. "It's the absolute truth, but it doesn't really matter what you believe."

Stacy's expression underwent another dramatic shift, eyes bulging as something important came to her. "No, no, no, hold the fuck on." She jabbed an emphatic finger in the singer's direction. "You don't *have* any fucking kids. Every interview I ever read, any time the subject came up, you always talked about how you never wanted any. Hell, I could swear you were still saying the same shit ten years ago." Her eyes flicked to the girl in a pointed way. "This one's, what, late teens? Doesn't add up."

Craig was surprised he hadn't thought of this, because while he hadn't kept up on news in the world of the Bile Lords or rock and roll in general in ages, he clearly recalled reading the same things down through the years. Kyle Bile famously espoused a total lack of interest in starting a family, having no taste for being tied down.

Kyle nodded. "You're not wrong, but the actual truth is I never had any *acknowledged* kids." He laughed. "Come on, think about it. I toured the whole world many times over and fucked countless groupies. You think none of them ever got knocked up? Mostly I paid them off and sent them on their way after making them sign an NDA. This one, though?" He ruffled Nona's hair again and she made a muffled sound of pitiful contentment. "She showed up on my doorstep a few months ago, claiming I was her daddy. I had a DNA test done. Sure enough, it came back positive."

Stacy's look of disbelieving indignation yielded to horror again. "If this isn't the most fucked up thing I've ever heard, I don't know what is. So, it turns out you have a daughter, one that sought you out, desperately wanted and needed your love, and instead of trying to give her a better life, your big idea is to sacrifice her to the fucking devil?"

Kyle rolled his eyes. "Again with the moral mundanity. I actually do truly love my long-lost little girl. Not just because she's my flesh and blood, but for her selfless willingness to do what's right for the sake of rock and roll. In case you hadn't noticed, real rock is dead as a force in popular culture, and it's up to the Bile Lords to bring it back."

He said this with a tone of rising drama.

Stacy and Craig looked at each other.

And they laughed.

Kyle scowled, real visible anger flaring inside him for the first time in a while. "Oh, you think that's funny? The idea of the Bile Lords as rock and roll saviors is ridiculous to you, is it?" He grunted. "I bet you were thinking something different just a little while ago. I watched you fuckers from the stage. Saw the adoration in your eyes. You looked like believers to me."

Craig nodded. "Yeah, you put on a good show. I'll give you that. But you didn't look like saviors of anything. You looked like a puffy has-been given a boost by energetic youngsters. What I think happened tonight was you put in extra effort to rise to the occasion this one time. You wanted to impress us and I guess you did. But you ain't got any hope of saving rock and roll, you delusional bag of blubber. The world has moved on, and no amount of sacrificing people to the devil will change that."

Kyle's face contorted with such violent rage that he looked for a moment like a guy in an 80s horror movie about to morph into a werewolf, veins throbbing everywhere. He flung his daughter away from him and charged at Craig too fast for him to react, raising a big fist that looked fully capable of meting out serious damage.

But the blow didn't come down.

Kyle's bottom lip trembled. An eyelid twitched. "I should kill you right now."

Craig smirked. "So do it. Stop running your useless trap for once in your life and just fucking do it."

Craig couldn't believe he'd said that.

The prospect of being violently killed held no more attraction for him than it normally did. A part of him was terrified to have uttered those words. And yet he was also glad he'd found the courage again to defy this deranged egomaniac. He'd already concluded he wasn't getting out of this situation alive, so he might as well go to his demise with a measure of dignity.

Over the course of interminable time, the singer's contorted, red-tinged features began to soften, bit by slow bit, the redness in his cheeks also doing a slow fade.

He backed off and managed a twitchy smile. "No. I won't let you play me that way. I'm not killing you yet because I still have plans for you." He shot a smirking glance at Stacy. "For both of you." He palmed sweat from his forehead, aiming a big grin at everyone. "Holy shit. Got myself all worked up there." He snapped his fingers and gestured at his lackeys. "All right, get these assholes out of here and back inside the club. I'll be out shortly."

The merch girl took this as her cue to take some of her boiling ire out on Stacy, hauling her up and twisting her arm behind her hard enough to make her screech in pain. The merch girl laughed and twisted her arm even harder.

The lanky guitarist waved the gun at Craig. "You too, man. On your feet. Let's go."

Craig grimaced as he heaved himself up. As he did this, the singer veered away from the group exiting the bus and lumbered his swaying way through the kitchenette before disappearing through the door in back. While the relatively lucid way he'd discussed his motivations for what was happening suggested he wasn't as blind drunk as he'd first seemed, that wasn't the gait of a sober person. Knowing his fate rested in the hands of a man who was both under the influence and mentally unwell inspired little in the way of hope that he and Stacy might yet survive this strange night.

Bill was directly in front of him as they departed the lounge. As they arrived at the steps leading out to the open two-panel side door and the parking lot beyond, he considered giving his old friend a hard shove in the back. He still didn't fully understand Bill's role in all this, though he could intuit some of it. What he *really* didn't understand was how a friend of such long-standing, one of the *closest* friends he'd ever had, could perpetrate a seeming betrayal of this magnitude.

The not knowing was the thing that stayed Craig's hand. Whatever the man had done or known in advance of the show, injuring him in some potentially serious way wasn't something he wanted on his conscience. Those decades of friendship still meant something to Craig, regardless of what was in the other man's head. Also, he was still hoping for a shade more enlightenment regarding what precisely he'd done and why.

Out in the back parking lot, a line of cars was now blocking the way into the lot from the little side street that went by the club. Not to further impede the possibility of escape, he presumed, but to fend off interlopers who might want to use the lot to turn around. Also, probably, to reduce the chances of passersby seeing something they shouldn't and reporting it to the police. Craig didn't need anyone to spell this out. It just made sense. It also deepened the many ominous implications regarding his and Stacy's fate.

They reached the rear door without incident and went into the backstage area. Out in the street, not so much as a single car had passed by during the time they'd spent out in the open. Not surprising, given the relative remoteness of the club's location and the lateness of the hour, which he now put at well past midnight. Yet another in a long list of bad luck things that didn't bode well.

The fluorescent ceiling lights flickered and buzzed as the procession clomped its way across threadbare old carpet discolored by innumerable ancient stains of mysterious origin. Spilled drinks, vomit, and various types of bodily fluids chief among them. An underlying odor of stale beer was baked into every inch of fiber and wood. As

Craig glanced to the left at a vanity mirror, he was assailed by another flashing glimpse of a rock and roll ghost, Jarrett sitting in the creaky wooden chair before the mirror, carefully applying his sleaze metal warpaint. Trying his hardest to look like a cross between Nikki Sixx and Stiv Bator. Which, honestly, was never one of his problems.

He always had the look down, as well as the attitude.

After emerging from the sad and tawdry backstage, they made their way to the open area in front of the stage, where they stopped. The club appeared to have shut down for the night. The yellow-tinged lighting was on, but no one was behind the bar and all the patrons had departed. Some special arrangement Kyle had made with the manager was the only explanation that came to mind. Made Craig wonder if the manager had any inkling of the true nature of this little after-hours party.

Probably not, but who could tell?

At the direction of the merch girl, the guitarist steered Craig to a spot about ten feet directly in front of the stage, where he was prompted to drop to his knees. Going to his knees without some means of levering himself back to his feet was not something he often did these days. Absent the aid of a cane, handy chair, or some other object he could grab onto, it was difficult as hell, sometimes bordering on impossible, but it seemed he had no choice.

With a tight grimace and a loud grunt of pain, he lowered himself to his knees with as much care as he could, the creaking of his old joints on the way down as loud as the snap of a stick on a snare drum.

Stacy was made to kneel next to him.

Craig turned his head to look at her, an old ache swelling in his chest at the sight of her puffy eyes and the tracks of tears continuing to spill. He could also see the beginnings of multiple bruises from the places where the merch girl's knuckles had connected with her face. As he reached for her trembling hand, she allowed him to take it, intertwining her fingers with his, squeezing for momentary comfort, if not reassurance.

He squeezed back.

The merch girl had a wadded-up piece of tissue wedged inside one nostril to stem the blood that'd erupted from being punched. When she smirked, it looked like it might come loose. "Aw, ain't that sweet? Little wrinkled lovebirds. Actually, it kind of makes me sick. Old people are gross."

Craig surprised himself with a laugh. "Speaking of gross, your face tampon is about to drop out."

Stacy cackled.

The merch girl's smirk did a quick fade. "Shoot these haggard-ass motherfuckers, Teddy."

The guitarist breathed a put-upon sigh, a sound Craig recognized as that of a person just about sick of putting up with another person's shit. "Can't do that." Now he sounded like a parent at the edge of losing patience with a spoiled, demanding child. "Not unless I have to. Definitely not for backtalk."

The merch girl sneeringly shook her head, but she didn't press the matter, instead turning her attention to Kyle's drugged-out daughter.

"Up on the stage, Nona."

The bleary-eyed ragamuffin looked at her in an unfocused way, head listing to one side as if it was too heavy to hold up straight. "Mm . . . is that where I make my sacrifice?"

The merch girl nodded. "Sure is. You excited?"

Nona made a sound that might have been a lazy indication of assent, but as fucked up as she was on whatever cocktail of drugs she was on, Craig wondered how real any of this was to her. Could a person who spent all their time in this kind of total haze consent in any meaningful way to offering up their own life in the name of some bullshit devil sacrifice ceremony?

He didn't think so, not that he had any say in it.

When Nona remained where she was, Rodney Cantor took her by an arm. She made a little sound of startlement and slight pain as he began pulling her toward the stage. Craig hoped this might be a first sign of second thoughts on her part, but when she allowed herself to be pulled along without further resistance, he muttered a profane expression of disappointment.

Stacy squeezed his hand.

A loud throat clearing from somewhere behind them made Craig turn his head, and he glowered when he saw Bill edging backward in the direction of the bar. Digging in his hip pocket, he started pulling out his phone as he said, "Hey, um, now that my part in this is done, I was thinking I'd book an Uber and head on out. That okay?"

He was looking right at the merch girl as he spoke, but it was Teddy who answered. "Not yet, man." The guitarist gestured with the gun, waving him back toward the area in front of the stage. "Kyle wants you here for the whole thing, you know that."

Bill slouched into a posture of disappointment, eyes blinking rapidly for a few moments, mouth moving without any sounds emerging as he tried to work out what to say next. Either he was afraid for his safety despite whatever deal he'd made with these people or he was too much of a coward to hang around and watch the friends he'd betrayed go to their deaths.

Or both.

Teddy became impatient and pointed the gun directly at Bill, tone shifting from his usual lazy slacker drawl to something harder as he said, "*Now*, dude. Get back over here and put that fucking phone in your pocket until this is over."

With obvious reluctance, Bill pocketed the phone and came away from the bar area. He moved with deliberate slowness, stopping at a spot several feet behind where Craig and Stacy knelt on the floor.

Craig suspected the traitor in their midst still had escape on his mind. His plan was probably to slip quietly away whenever the next opportunity arose, this time without asking permission. In his place, Craig supposed he'd be hedging his bets in similar fashion. These people he'd conspired with were unstable and not to be trusted. With multiple acts of murder already likely to take place here tonight, wouldn't it make sense to eliminate anyone with direct knowledge of what happened? He couldn't help thinking Bill might only just now have started taking that possibility into account.

Leaving aside the seemingly nonexistent possibility of escape for himself and Stacy, the one thing Craig wanted most before being murdered was fuller, more explicit knowledge of what Bill had done and why he'd done it.

Still on his knees, he twisted his torso around to fix Bill with a look that was one part smoldering rage and one part brokenhearted curiosity.

"You were the lure, weren't you?" Craig nodded, because this was the more obvious part of it, the bit he'd already hashed out in his mind. "Sure you were. That text you sent me a week ago, the picture of the flyer, that wasn't as random as you made it out to be, was it? If not for that, we wouldn't be here tonight."

That made the merch girl chuckle. "You'd be here no matter what, asshole. If things hadn't worked out with your Benedict Arnold of a friend, Kyle would've figured out some other way of getting you here."

Craig ignored her while silently accepting the likely truth of the assertion. His gaze remained on Bill as he uttered his next words.

"Why the hell did you do it? We're your *friends*." He nearly choked on the word *friends*, voice hoarsening from an impending sob. "Your oldest, closest friends. How could you do this?"

At first Bill flinched at the harshness of his tone and looked away, but then he looked him in the eye and said, "You don't really believe that. Do you?" His mouth twisted in a bitter half-sneer. "*Closest* friends? Really?" He made a scoffing sound, shook his head. "Maybe way back in the day that was sort of almost true, but you need to take off your rose-colored nostalgia glasses. We've barely been real friends at all for a long time. Before today, when was the last time we saw each other? Six months ago? Longer? Hell, we went one period of three, almost four years without so much as a single email or text, and in the end, it was me who broke the silence, like usual. Shit, I only let it go that long to see how long you'd hold out. My guess? If I hadn't reached out, you would have been content *never* hearing from me again." A heavier note of sarcasm entered his tone. "Closest fucking friends. Give me a break."

The vehemence and vitriol of this reply—not to mention its extended nature, itself highly unusual for Bill—left Craig temporarily incapable of an immediate response. They stared at each other in seething silence for close to a minute while Craig grappled with the towering resentment that had sharpened the man's every word to a razor's edge. Words that cut to his core. In his darkest imaginings, he'd never thought Bill's good-humored outward persona masked anything like this level of bitterness.

Ultimately, it was Stacy who broke the silence, after sensing Craig was still too shocked by Bill's accusations to speak up in his defense. "Grow up, Bill," she said, shifting toward him while still on her knees. "My God, you sound like a petulant child. People get old and they grow apart. That's life. And it sure as shit isn't a legit excuse for what you've done."

The merch girl giggled. "Ooh, old people drama. It's like a geriatric version of *Love Island* or some shit, only with no sexy people and not on a fucking island. Call it *Real Old Farts of Bumfuck, Nowhere,* maybe."

Teddy chuckled. "I can dig it. All that's missing is some popcorn."

The merch girl snorted. "Nah, a pint of Haagen-Das. Curled up on a comfy couch, gorging myself, high as fuck, watching my new favorite show."

Teddy nodded. "And at the end of each episode, one of the old fucks gets voted off the show, only instead of going home they walk into a euthanasia booth and wave goodbye through a little window while it fills with gas."

The merch girl nodded, giggling again. "Brilliant. Fucking brilliant. Dude, I'd fuck you right now just for coming up with that shit if I didn't think Kyle would kill me for it."

Teddy's smile faded as she said this, lips pursing and brow furrowing as he looked away from her.

The silence that followed was short-lived as Bill erupted in rage, face reddening and spittle flying from the corners of his mouth. "You assholes want an explanation? Fine, here it is. The two of you are the most self-centered people I've ever known. I'm so sick of the way the shadow of your great failed romance hangs over everything, even all these goddamn years later, as if you're Romeo and Juliet or Sid and Nancy, when the truth is you're just a couple of ordinary nobodies. But worse than all that is the thing you've both been too blind to ever see."

Silence again, Bill's face redder than ever as he eyed them with an air of expectant contempt.

Feeling the onset of a headache, Craig said, "Just let it out. Whatever this bullshit is you've been holding in. Get it out of your system while we're all still alive, because I don't think that's gonna be the case much longer."

Bill spat on the floor. "You're the reason it happened. Both of you."

The corners of Craig's eyes crinkled in confusion. "The reason *what* happened?"

Bill sneered. "Jarrett killed himself because of you."

Stacy shook her head. "Didn't that idiot singer just tell us Jarrett offed himself in the name of the Bile Lords? Are you saying that's not true?"

"I'm not saying that, no. Jarrett *did* do that. But the *bigger* truth is he was driven to it by the indifference of the people he cared most about. By which I mean the two of you." Bill held up a hand, warding off their automatic indignant protests. "The stories you've built up in your heads to let yourselves off the hook are *lies.*" His eyes locked on Craig before uttering his next words. "We all went to the funeral, didn't we? Cried and hugged. Had beers and shared memories at the bar after. But you never said a word about how neither of you had talked to him for five fucking years by the time he put that noose around his neck. Did you?"

Tears welled in Craig's eyes. "You asshole. You *know* there were reasons for that. *Good* reasons."

Stacy glared at Bill. "*Damn* good reasons. Things he said. Things he did. He was *fucked up*."

Bill nodded. "Yeah. He was. And he needed help. Needed his friends. I knew about his letters to Kyle. Writing those was his outlet, his way of venting all his pain. He never told either of you because he was afraid of what you'd think, that you'd see it as pathetic loser behavior." He laughed in a flat, bitter way. "I mean, even those times when the man he worshipped, his idol, actually responded to him with a letter or phone call, something he was so excited about, he never said shit about it to either of you out of fear of the condescending way he knew you'd react. Poor guy was always so desperate for your approval. God knows why." He shook his head. "Jarrett didn't commit suicide. Not really. You murdered him. You ask how I could do this to you? *That's* why."

The merch girl let out a long, low whistle. "Wow. I already didn't like you motherfuckers on general principle, but you really do *suuuuuuck*."

Teddy again gestured with the gun. "Enough already. You people aren't resolving your issues tonight, or ever, so shut up already. Turn back around. Eyes toward the stage."

Craig complied with the directive even as he continued to stew over the many unfair things Bill had said. By leaving out the excellent reasons they'd often had for keeping their distance from Jarrett for extended periods, Bill had painted a deceptive picture. They'd done what they'd done to maintain their own peace and mental health, and it wasn't just them. Several other former close friends and associates had gone to great lengths to avoid Jarrett, including one former girlfriend who'd taken out a restraining order against him. He'd long had a habit, one that got worse in his later years, of being emotionally abusive and making drunken threats. Bill had been right about one thing. The guy had needed help, serious professional help, but he'd always refused it, sometimes in explosively angry ways. At a certain point, all you could do was cut ties and hope the guy eventually got his head screwed on straight.

Unfortunately, it never happened.

Bill *knew* that.

And yet here he was, heaping this bullshit guilt trip on them.

It was insane.

Nona was on her knees in the center of the stage, in the same approximate spot where her father had spent much of his time rocking out earlier in the evening, giving a performance that had thrilled a small contingent of old fans. Most of whom had gone home and tomorrow would tell stories gushing with excitement about how Kyle Bile had summoned some semblance of the rock god he'd once been to deliver a performance for the ages.

You should've been there, they'd say.

And for them it'd be true.

As for Craig, he wished like hell he'd missed out on it.

Standing behind Nona was Rodney Cantor, whose thin frame, weathered skin, and leaning posture made him look like a scarecrow dressed all in black. On the floor directly in front of Nona was a large plastic bucket. In his right hand, Rodney held a big hunting knife with a long, serrated blade.

Craig thought, *Fuck, they're really gonna do it, sacrifice this poor girl in the name of an almost certainly nonexistent entity for a really stupid reason.*

He was still thinking about that when the door at the side of the stage was thrown open and Kyle Bile at last rejoined the party. Trailing behind him was the rest of his young backing band and the other roadie, all of them wearing either neutral or carefully guarded expressions. Craig figured they didn't all share the same level of enthusiasm for becoming accessories to murder, despite tacitly approving by going along with it.

In the time he'd remained behind on the bus, Kyle had changed back into his stage clothes, only now the buttoned-up leather vest he wore over his otherwise bare torso looked tighter than it had earlier, as if he'd somehow gained another five pounds around the gut just since the end of the show. Clutched in one hand was the neck of another whiskey bottle, a third of its contents already drained.

The other members of Kyle's entourage joined the little group in front of the stage while Kyle vaulted himself onto it from the side. He was fortunate the stage was a mere two feet or so above the level of the floor, because as it was, the toe of one of his boots clipped the edge of the modestly elevated platform. He stumbled and came within an eyelash of an embarrassing spill, but through some miracle he was able to avoid this fate and remain upright.

He laughed as he staggered right up to the front edge of the stage, again displaying a sloppy, drunken lack of spatial awareness, coming maybe an inch away from going over the edge and faceplanting on the floor. Swilling whiskey, he took a shuffling backward step.

"Damn, I might be a little fucked up."

The comment drew a couple of halfhearted laughs from his crew.

After yet another big swig of whiskey, the singer said, "I feel like this whole ceremony thing, the ritual or whatever, is a little underproduced. Like, at the very least I should've come in with some proper entrance music playing. 'The Imperial March' or 'Ride of the Valkyries', some kind of grandiose shit like that. Maybe have some dry ice mist on the stage. Fuck." He wheeled about in his staggering way and glared at Rodney. "Feels like that kind of thing should fall under your purview. You let me down, man."

Rodney smiled, shrugging. "Sorry about that, boss. You want me to go see if I can put something on the sound system?"

Kyle appeared to consider this a moment before waving off the idea. "No, fuck it. The sooner we get this done, the sooner I can go crash for about twelve hours." He turned toward the front of the stage again, reapproaching the edge with a bit more caution than before. After a bleary-eyed scan of all the faces looking up at him, his gaze settled on Craig and Stacy. "There they are. The guests of dishonor."

Another token few chuckles from the sycophants in the audience.

Kyle took a smaller swallow from his bottle. "You're in the position you're in tonight, both of you, so I can do right by my boy Jarrett while also giving my band the juice it needs so it can rise again and reclaim its proper place in the rock and roll pantheon." He did a half-turn away from them but then turned back fast, a look of drunken mischief on his face. "But wait, there's a twist!"

The mischievous look endured a bit longer, but it faltered when the subsequent silence began to stretch out. During the silence, someone coughed. Soon someone else cleared their throat. Craig perceived a building tension even among Kyle's bandmates and crew, a few of them exchanging furtive looks of puzzlement. Then he realized the singer was upset because no one had prompted him to elaborate on the twist, like a performer awaiting a cue that never came.

Craig groaned. "This isn't Broadway, asshole. Just spit it out."

One of the newly arrived members of Kyle's entourage tried—and failed—to stifle a laugh.

Kyle scowled. "The *twist* is that I'm offering one of you pieces of shit a chance to walk out of here with your blood still on the inside, instead of spilled out all over the floor. But, man, I don't know, if you're just gonna say mean shit like that, maybe I should rescind the offer. What do you think, Craigy-poo?"

Craig thought the man had some serious fucking balls to complain about any "mean shit" directed his way, considering that mean shit was practically all that ever came out of his mouth.

He shrugged. "I don't think I can tell you what I think without hearing more details. Also, I don't know how enticing any offer could be that's only being extended to one of us."

Kyle pointed at him with the index finger of the hand holding the whiskey bottle. "See, though, that's the whole point. Sacrifice. What this ritual is all about. I'm already offering up the life of my only verified offspring, which by itself is powerful fuel for dark magic." He chuckled and again crept closer to the front of the stage. "But if we mix in other forms of sacrifice, both of the spirit and the flesh, it becomes even more potent. We do this right, the Bile Lords are heading all the way back to the top. Sold-out arenas again, new chart hits, the sky's the fucking limit. Shit, maybe even a biopic loaded with A-listers."

Stacy laughed. "You're delusional, man."

Kyle responded with mocking laughter of his own. "That's some mouth you got on you, bitch. I've got something that'll shut you up right here." He grabbed his crotch and made a thrusting gesture with his pelvis. "What do you think, honey? Wanna choke on some rock star splooge?"

Stacy's face twisted in disgust. "I think I'd rather swallow cyanide."

"Whatever. You know you want it, you skanky old witch." His gaze landed on Craig again. "Okay, details. You see that big-ass knife my man Rodney has? Looks wicked sharp, right? Well, trust me, it is. It could almost cut through steel. Seriously. It'll damn sure cut through my daughter's throat like butter. Won't it, Rodster?"

Rodney nodded. "Sure will, boss."

The singer smiled. "What I'm offering is simple. If one of you, doesn't matter who, volunteers to bend Nona's head over that bucket and unzip her throat so that she bleeds out into it, the other one goes free."

"Neither of us is doing that. Even if we believed you, which we don't, it's not happening. You'll have to do your own dirty work. Right, Craig?" Stacy looked at him when he failed to respond. "*Right*,

Craig?"

Craig was in a staring contest with Kyle Bile. A part of him instinctively understood this offer wasn't truly being extended to either of them, because it was a given that Stacy, who'd always been made of sturdier moral fiber, would never consent to such abhorrent terms.

"Just so I understand, if I do this, I'd be killed after the deed is done."

Kyle nodded. "Yes, and by agreeing, you'll be sacrificing not only your life but your soul. By acting as my instrument, you'll amplify the power of the ritual. As a native-born son of Drayton Falls, a place where the ground is cursed and the bloodlines carry seeds of darkness down through the generations, as good ol' Jarrett put it once upon a time, I'm betting the spilling of your blood might turn this thing into a motherfucking dark magic atom bomb."

Craig made a noise of contemplation, nodding a single time.

Stacy smacked him in the arm. "*Craig!* You can't seriously be thinking of doing this."

Craig said nothing.

Stacy screeched in exasperation. "Goddammit, Craig, listen to me and listen good. You don't get to make some stupid grand gesture on my behalf, especially not when the terms are so fucking evil. If you do, I'll curse your name forever. I'll haunt you in hell, I swear to fucking Christ. More than that, you'll make me hate you. *Please* don't do that."

The plaintiveness of what she was saying tore at Craig, but maybe he'd have to harden his heart and accept her hating him. Maybe it'd be worth that if he could extricate her from this nightmare.

"If I do this, what guarantee do I have that you'll do as you say and let her go?"

Kyle shrugged. "Well, man, you'll be dead, so you won't actually know, but I give you my word. My solemn vow. Act as my instrument in the ritual, fulfill what I have asked of you, and she'll be released unharmed."

Stacy sighed. "Craig, you are not a stupid man. You've got to see that this man can't be trusted. The second your body hits the floor, he'll have me killed, too. Because he's not stupid either. He knows if he lets me go, I'll head straight to the police and tell them everything."

Kyle laughed, still mostly keeping his gaze on the person he was trying to convince. "What your bitch isn't understanding is that I'm an old pro at this. This ain't even close to my first blood ritual rodeo.

I've got bodies buried all over the highways and byways of this country. It's what I've had to do to keep the band going during all the lean years. What I'm saying is, we'll make all the evidence disappear. Anyone she tells about this will just think she's crazy. And we'll just move on down the line to the next show and the next town."

A brief silence.

Then Stacy grabbed his arm and squeezed hard. "Craig, look at me."

Craig kept his gaze straight ahead and said nothing for several seconds.

He came to a decision.

The next step would be to look at Stacy and tell her that he loved her and had always loved her, that even so she was free to hate him, and that he hoped one day she could accept why he'd made the choice he had.

The next step after that would be to ask for help getting to his feet.

So he could go to the stage and do what he had to do, as much as it made him sick to his stomach. It would be awful, the worst thing he'd ever done or ever considered doing by a magnitude of thousands, but somehow he would look deep inside himself and find the strength to do it.

Except that he never did any of that.

Because before he could say yes to the singer's diabolical proposition, a familiar voice, one that shook him to his core to hear in this place, under these horrific circumstances, spoke up from somewhere behind him. He also heard footsteps approaching from behind, coming at an unhurried but steady pace.

Craig shifted around on his knees again and saw Janine coming toward them from the direction of the bar. Seeing his wife in this grungy, dimly lit rock and roll club was almost as strange as any of the other many strange things that had happened on this, the most bizarre and terrifying night of his life.

"Nobody's killing that girl tonight, Craig, least of all you."

Craig was in too much of a state of disbelief to have any idea how to respond to that. He kept staring at Janine with an uncomprehending deep frown, as if he expected her to disappear at any moment, revealed as a last-minute hallucination conjured by an overstressed brain pushed to the breaking point.

Kyle snuffed out that idea when he said, "Who is this bitch and who let her in?"

Janine smirked. "I let myself in. The front door was open."

She was wearing a fitted denim jacket over a long pink dress with a hemline that hit just below the knee and shiny red boots. A small handbag dangled from her shoulder by a long strap. Her right hand was inside the open bag, and Craig had a feeling her fingers were wrapped around the slim cylindrical pepper spray can she carried with her wherever she went. A thing like that might be effective against a single assailant at close range, but what she hoped to accomplish with it in this situation, he did not know.

Unless, of course, she'd come here to spray it in his face as retribution for ignoring the text she'd sent. It was the kind of thing an angry wife might do when confronting her husband after discovering incriminating evidence of possible marital misbehavior, though reactions of that sort were not typical of Janine. Craig supposed it was possible his failure to respond had pushed her over the edge. He guessed it was also possible he'd underestimated the true depth of his wife's resentment of his old girlfriend.

A fresh dose of stress-triggered adrenaline helped Craig find the strength to get up on one knee as Janine continued to come closer. "Jeannie, I'm sorry I didn't get back to you earlier, but you need to get out of here right now."

Janine shook her head. "Oh, fuck off with your apologies. I don't care about any of that right now, and I'm not going anywhere yet."

"Craig's right," Stacey implored her. "You need to get out of here while you can. These are bad people."

Janine regarded Stacy with the kind of look people normally reserve for encountering especially gross piles of vomit or shit on the sidewalk. "You can fuck off too, slut."

Up on the stage, Kyle laughed, belatedly getting the gist of the situation. "Okay, so the spurned wifey has joined the party. Awesome. This changes the ritual equation in a potentially really interesting way." He turned his head, flipping his long hair out of his face, and looked at Teddy. "Get that bitch up here, man."

Craig's heart started pounding harder. "No."

He braced a hand on Stacy's shoulder and used it to propel himself shakily to his feet.

Teddy breathed his typical put-upon sigh as he pushed away from the thick wooden support beam he'd been leaning against and began to lazily raise his revolver.

"Okay, lady, let's—"

Janine's hand came out of her bag.

She was not holding a can of pepper spray.

Teddy stopped in his tracks, gaping at the small semi-automatic pistol gripped in her hand. The gun was aimed straight at his chest. "Um . . . shit."

He appeared to be considering the relative wisdom of getting his own gun properly aimed at his opponent.

Janine shook her head. "Don't even think about it. Pop that cylinder out and empty the bullets onto the floor, then drop that fucking thing."

"Don't you dare listen to that bitch!" Kyle shouted from the stage, gesturing in an emphatic way with the hand holding the whiskey bottle, causing amber liquid to slop out of it. "Just shoot the cunt."

Teddy's gaze went to the unwavering muzzle of Janine's pistol.

He opened the revolver's cylinder. A moment later, bullets began clattering on the floor. When he was done, he tossed the empty weapon away, putting enough force into it to send it sliding under one of the tables in the tiny dining area.

Kyle threw up his hands and shouted again: "Un-fucking-believable! Why the hell did you do that?"

Teddy shrugged and dug out a pack of cigarettes and a lighter. "Pretty sure I'd be dead by now if I hadn't," he said, wedging a smoke into a corner of his mouth and lighting up. "There's a lot I'm willing to do in the name of rock and roll. Getting shot isn't one of them."

In his own way, Craig figured he was at least as flabbergasted by these developments as Kyle sounded. Janine showing up unexpectedly was a surprise, but her taking out a gun he hadn't even known she owned was a much bigger shock. Even more unsettling was the matter of *why* she'd brought the weapon with her to the club. After all, she'd had no idea she would be walking into a situation as unusual and dangerous as this one.

Had she come here to kill him, maybe even Stacy?

That didn't strike him as the kind of thing Janine would ever even think about doing, even at her most enraged.

Yet, there was the gun.

And she'd made a conscious decision to bring it here.

So . . .

Craig shuddered. "Jeannie, I'm s-sorry . . . I never meant . . ."

Janine rolled her eyes. "Spare me the apologies. I know what it looks like, but I'm not here to kill you." She glanced at Stacy, scowling. "You either, bitch."

Kyle reared an arm back and slung it forward, sending the almost empty whiskey bottle sailing high over everyone's heads. An instant later, it shattered on the floor behind the bar. "Fuck this!" He turned and staggered over to the center of the stage, where he snatched the big hunting knife away from Rodney. Shoving the old roadie out of the way, he seized a handful of his whimpering daughter's hair, pulled her head roughly backward, and put the long blade against her slender throat. "Nothing's stopping the ritual! *Nothing*!"

Janine's expression didn't change as she turned calmly in the direction of the singer, took perhaps one full second to size up her aim, and squeezed the trigger. The percussive boom of the gun's report was loud in the small space and Craig flinched hard enough to make his body seize up in a painful way.

On the stage, Kyle's head snapped sharply backward and then came forward again as he remained upright a single beat longer. A dime-sized hole leaked blood from the center of his forehead. A good deal more blood had splashed the back of the stage behind him.

Then he collapsed to the stage and didn't move.

The merch girl screamed with such ear-shredding volume it hurt Craig's ears more than either the gunshot or the high-decibel rock and roll show he'd watched earlier in the evening.

She screamed again, somehow even louder this second time.

She turned and charged straight at Janine.

Janine swung the gun around and fired again, this time sending a bullet through the girl's left bicep, a non-lethal wound that was nonetheless debilitating enough to drop her instantly to the floor, where she moaned and writhed in agony.

Stacy heaved a breath. "Holy shit, goddamn."

Janine turned her attention back to the freshly disarmed guitarist. "Listen close, because I'm going to tell you something and you need to decide fast. Ordinarily, the thing to do here would be to call the cops and let them sort all this shit out, but I just killed a kind of famous guy with a gun that isn't mine. I don't want the attention or trouble those things would bring." She cast a meaningful glance around, being sure she had the attention of everyone else in Kyle Bile's entourage. "My impression is the guy I killed was the driving force behind all of this. Call it a hunch, but I get the feeling the rest of you would also prefer to put this behind you and avoid law enforcement scrutiny. Correct?"

After eyeing each other, there was a general murmur of agreement among the band members and crew.

Janine nodded. "I thought as much. So here's what I propose. We all get the fuck out of here and go our own way. We never see each other again and never breathe a word of this to anyone. That work for everybody?"

More nods and murmurs of agreement.

She looked at Teddy. "What about you? Planning on being a source of trouble if I let you go?"

He exhaled a big cloud of smoke. "No ma'am. The only thing I care about at this point is getting as far away from this place as possible and staying away. Forever. Your plan gets a big thumbs-up from me."

The squirming merch girl moaned from the floor. "She killed Kyle." A loud sob distorted her voice. "Kill her. Fucking *kill* her."

Another tired sigh from the guitarist. "I guess I just don't see the point, girl. With Kyle gone, none of this matters anymore. Without him, we're just a tribute band. I think maybe it's time to cut my hair and get into the emo scene. I hear that shit still does pretty well on the county fair retread circuit."

The girl whimpered. "But I loved him."

Teddy shook his head. "No, you didn't. You loved fucking somebody who used to be famous. That's all. But you'll get over it."

He dropped his half-smoked cigarette on the floor and began walking away, headed in the direction of the open door at the side of the stage.

The rest of the entourage followed after a brief hesitation. A couple of them—the chubbier of the two roadies and one of the band members—veered first toward the fallen merch girl, helping her to her feet even as she continued to whimper in pain and bemoan Kyle's fate. Working together, though, they were able to get her moving in the right direction and soon they were also gone.

Rodney Cantor came down from the stage and approached Craig and the rest of his group while holding his hands up, signaling peaceful intentions. Craig remained wary. This was, after all, a man who'd worked closely with Kyle for nearly forty years. They'd killed his boss and meal ticket. He'd also played a significant role in arranging the circumstances of their near demise, and there was ample evidence of him being a bad guy in other ways, such as the dazed young girl still kneeling on the stage. It seemed prudent to suspect he was still a danger.

Craig was not unhappy when Janine turned her gun Cantor's way. He had a hunch she would not hesitate to put a bullet between his eyes at the slightest indication of nefarious intent. The thought was reassuring on one level, but a part of him was still freaked out that she had a gun at all after decades of expressing nothing but disdain for firearms. That she also seemed to be a crack shot only deepened the mystery, as did her claim that the weapon didn't belong to her. There were troubling implications to these things, but the bottom line was she'd saved his life—and Stacy's life—and he was grateful for that.

Rodney smiled. "You can relax, folks. I just wanted to let you know you don't need to fear any future blowback from tonight's events. I'll make sure the exact circumstances of this . . ." He hooked a thumb over his shoulder to indicate the corpse on the stage. ". . . remain forever unknown."

Stacy said, "A coverup. You really believe you'll be able to pull that off?"

He shrugged, smile broadening. "I have experience in that area, so yeah." He laughed in a disquieting way. "Trust me, I'll be able to gin up a scenario about an unknown obsessed fan shooter, something the cops will buy. The three of you will be able to go about your lives as if none of this ever happened."

Craig frowned.

The three of you.

He turned his head and saw that Bill was gone, having at last managed to slip away, presumably at some point during the chaos that ensued following Janine's arrival.

That squirrely little weasel.

He'd have to deal with the man at some point. In some definitive way. Not only had he left them in the lurch, he'd drawn them into a situation in which the expectation was that they would die. You didn't get to just walk away from something like that like it never happened.

But that was a worry for another day.

His attention returned to Kyle's former right-hand man. "You're acting like you're not even upset that your boss is dead. Why is that?"

Rodney chuckled. "Kyle was never my boss, even if I let him behave like he was. That deal with the devil he talked about? That was real, but the truth is a little different from what he let on. Lucifer himself would never deal directly with someone of such minor importance as a mid-level rock and roller. Maybe he'd deign to take an audience with someone like an Axl Rose or Mick Jagger at the height of their fame and influence, but someone like Kyle, who was basically just a somewhat successful copycat?" A smirk as he shook his head. "Not a chance. That's not to say people like Kyle don't have their uses in the infernal scheme of things. They do. It's just that he farms out minor league shit like that to his representatives on earth. Here. Let me show you something."

The old roadie placed his hands against the sides of his head and pressed his fingers hard against his temples. His face twisted in pain and a moment later a pair of horns pushed through the flesh at the top of his forehead.

Stacy gasped in shock and slapped a hand over mouth.

Craig gulped. "Oh, shit. What the fuck?"

Janine squinted. "Are those real? They can't be. Can they?'

"Of course they're real. Watch this." Rodney covered the horns with his palms, making noises of discomfort as he pressed down on them. When he took his hands away, they'd disappeared back into his head. "That ain't no special effect. This isn't a movie. You saw what you think you saw."

Stacy's hand came away from her mouth. "You're a . . . what, a demon?"

Rodney waggled a hand in the air. "Mm, something like that. The point is, while I've enjoyed the ride with Kyle, it was never anything more than an entertaining pit stop along the long and winding highway to hell. Kyle's dead. So what? I'll move on to the next gullible soul willing to accept my help for a shot at fortune and fame. Meanwhile, I'll profit immensely from Kyle's tragic end. You know how it is. When old rock stars die, their sales go up. I think you can multiply the usual death bump by a factor of at least ten when that death comes as the result of a mysterious unsolved murder. And of course cutting myself in on a piece of the action is always part of the deals I make."

Craig stared at the man's forehead, searching for evidence of the holes created by the emergence of the horns, but all evidence they'd ever been there had vanished. Not so much as a speck of blood remained. Even stranger, he looked years younger, some of the deepest of his wrinkles dissolving away as they stood there talking with him.

Janine cleared her throat. "I don't fully understand what's going on here, but I think we should all leave now."

Rodney nodded, his grin bigger and scarier than ever. "An excellent idea."

Craig glanced toward the girl still kneeling on the stage. "What about her? We can't just leave her with . . . an agent of hell."

Agent of hell.

Craig doubted he'd ever sincerely uttered words as absurd as those at any previous point in his life, but what else would he call the guy?

Rodney's grin was replaced by a twitching scowl of gut-curdling intensity. His forehead appeared to swell and become more prominent. "Don't you worry about her. She will come to no harm any time soon." A flicker of that former grin twitched the corners of his mouth. "With the passing of her father, I have new ideas for the poor little lady, means of profiting from her tale of woe. The possibilities are endless. A prime-time reveal of her identity. The usual talk show circuit. A revealing and scandalous interview with *Rolling Stone.* A bestselling book, maybe even that biopic Kyle dreamed of." A meaningful pause as his features hardened again. "I'd advise against attempting to interfere with any of that."

Craig just stared at him, frowning, unsure how to respond.

Janine returned the pistol to her handbag and grabbed him by an arm. "Let's go."

Craig allowed himself to be pulled away.

He didn't much care for the idea of the profoundly vulnerable girl remaining behind in the care of a . . . demon . . . or whatever . . . but it was clear he had little choice in the matter.

Stacy followed them out to the club's front parking lot.

The three of them stood in the middle of the lot, taking wary measure of each other for several moments, none of them quite seeming to know what to do next.

Craig frowned. "About the gun . . ."

Janine's expression was flinty, her tone defiant as she said, "What about it?"

His frown deepened and he swallowed with some difficulty. "What was your plan in bringing it to the club? Were you going to kill us?"

Janine appeared wounded by that, the look on her face softening as her eyes brimmed with tears. "Do you really think I could do that?"

Craig's mind flashed back to her shooting Kyle. The way she swung the gun around without hesitation and killed him with a single shot.

Appearing to sense his thoughts, she grimaced, shaking her head. "I don't know, Craig, I was upset. I had some drinks and started spiraling." She wiped tears away. "So I got dressed and came out here. I think all I wanted to do was make a scene and ruin your night, the same way you ruined mine." The tears started coming faster. "Maybe at the most I would have waved the gun around to scare you so you could see how upset I really was."

Stacy said, "Just brandishing a gun in a public place can get you sent to jail."

"When I want your input, bitch, I'll ask for it."

Craig grunted. "She's right, though. Where did you even get it? You said it wasn't yours?"

"I took it off a weird guy I met on Tinder."

The blunt way she said it, with a defiant lift of her chin, caught Craig off-guard, like an invisible blow to the solar plexus.

She nodded. "That's right. You're not the only one with secrets. It only happened the one time months ago and I didn't enjoy it, if that means anything to you. I was at a really low point, just fucking sad about everything. I don't even know why I swiped his gun and booked it out of there while he was sleeping. I just did."

Craig rubbed a hand across his face, feeling more bleary-eyed and tired by the moment. He had a headache and his stomach was churning from all the excitement and stress. On top of all that, the pain in his back and knees from being made to kneel on that concrete floor was excruciating. There seemed little point in continuing to interrogate his wife about the gun.

"I'm sorry I've been such a shit," he told her, saying it with every ounce of sincerity he could muster. "Truly. I should have told you Stacy would be with us tonight. And if you'd objected, I shouldn't have gone. Hell, she said as much when I told her what I'd done."

Janine wiped more tears from her face and looked directly at Stacy for the first time. "Did you really?"

Stacy nodded, her reply coming in a soft monotone. "I did."

Janine sighed. "Well . . . we'll never be friends, but I thank you for that."

After that, it was decided that Craig would drive Stacy home and drop her off, after which he'd return to his own home and his wife. What went unsaid in that moment was any mention of the long talk they would then have to have about so many things, among them their future and whether they even still had one together.

When Janine got in her car and drove away, Craig stood there and watched until it disappeared from sight. As soon as that happened, he and Stacy got in his car, music assailing their ears as he turned the key in the ignition. *Hollywood Babylon* by the Bile Lords, the CD they'd been listening to on the way to the show.

A lifetime ago, seemingly.

Craig hit the radio's power button, cutting off the music.

They drove mostly in silence all the way back to Stacy's place, which wasn't far away, while the house where he and Janine lived was on the far side of town, in a much nicer neighborhood. When he pulled up in front of her house, he expected her to immediately exit with only the tersest of goodbyes, perhaps without saying a single word.

Instead she remained there in the passenger seat and exhaled the longest and weariest sigh Craig had ever heard.

Then she reached over and took him by the hand, squeezing it with real affection. "I'm sorry, babe, but I don't know if we should ever see each other again."

His eyes misted. "I don't know, either." He squeezed her hand back. Then he laughed, but not in a happy way, his bleary eyes looking out the windshield. "You know, this is the part of the movie where the star-crossed lovers always say fuck everything and drive off into the sunset together for one last shot at living happily ever after. Some upbeat song on the radio as the credits roll."

Stacy nodded. "I know. And I'd be lying if I said there wasn't some part of me that wishes we could do that." She squeezed his hand again. "But I think we both know better. The time when we could have just run away together is long gone. And if I've learned anything from this crazy night, it's about the value in letting go."

Craig sobbed.

Stacy leaned over and kissed him on the cheek. She put a hand to the back of his head and another on his knee, and they sat there in silence as she held him like that a little longer. Then she put her mouth close to his ear and whispered words of consolation. "Listen. Life isn't like the movies. Things don't get worked out in ninety minutes of runtime, all your issues resolved neat and tidy. The only thing we know about the future is the end we all get sooner or later. Go home and talk to your wife. See what happens. Maybe you split, maybe you don't. Even if you do, there's so much else to think about. Your kid, my kids. The guy I've been kind of seeing lately." She sighed. "I don't even know what *I* want. But just remember, whatever anyone else says, you're a good guy. Not perfect, but good, deep down. And your wife isn't some flawless angel, either. You got all the proof you'll ever need of that tonight. Do what's right for you, okay?"

He opened his mouth to tell her to stay, but the words wouldn't come.

Stacy touched his cheek. "Goodbye, Craig."

She pushed away from him, moving fast as she got out of his car and threw the door shut behind her before he could reply. Craig turned his head and through his tears watched her as she crossed the yard, climbed the steps to her porch, opened the door, and stepped inside.

He stared at the closed door for at least a full minute, and while he did, he thought a bit more about his long ago, misspent youth and all the many ways he'd fucked up. He thought again about some of the things that had happened over the course of the night, including revelations he could happily have gone many lifetimes without knowing, and the impossibility of changing any of it.

The past is gone. Move along, old man.

Craig put his car in gear and pulled away from the curb. As he picked up speed and made his way through the dark streets of Stacy's neighborhood, he hit the button to lower the driver's side window.

As he exited the neighborhood, he ejected the Bile Lords CD from the player and whipped it out the window.

Driving faster, he felt for the CD case, found it, broke it in half, and tossed that out, too.

It was strange how much lighter he felt in the moments that followed.

It was like an exorcism.

Rock and roll was forever and he would love it until his dying breath, but Stacy was right. About many things, but one thing in particular. Sometimes it was okay to let go of things you loved.

Or even just *thought* you'd loved.

Like the fucking Bile Lords.

DIGGING UP EMILY

TEN NIGHTS AFTER MURDERING HIS girlfriend and burying her in the woods behind his house, Aden Withers donned black clothing, strapped on a backpack, grabbed his shovel and flashlight, and ventured out into the chilly evening to return to the burial site.

A part of him still couldn't believe he'd killed Emily. He knew it was a thing that had happened. There was no delusion on that count. It was just that in the time between the night of the murder and this night, he'd compartmentalized the grisly event in such thorough fashion he'd been able to put it almost entirely out of his head. A vague awareness of what he'd done flickered at the edges of consciousness a few times over the course of that strange stretch of days, but these moments were no more consequential than the buzzing of a fly around his head. Each time they occurred, he banished the thoughts back into the murky depths of his subconscious with a twitch of his head so minute he was barely aware of it.

Then tonight, just a short while ago, it'd all come flooding back, every gory detail, as if a switch had been thrown in his mind. The woman in black had told him it would be that way that day at the diner, after she'd convinced him of the necessity of murdering the love of his life. It was part of the spell she'd cast, a failsafe of sorts to prevent him from becoming overcome with regret and remorse. All in the name of allowing the magic the time it needed to work as intended.

Thinking about the woman in black as he neared the tree line behind his house made him shiver in a way that wasn't just to do with the chilly night air. He'd never met her until the moment she'd slipped into the opposite side of the booth where he and Emily had just finished having their breakfast. This was within seconds of Emily getting up to go to the bathroom. The woman's sudden presence was startling for multiple reasons, its abrupt and unexpected nature being merely the first of them.

Prior to her departure, Emily had spent several minutes delivering a harsh and hurtful critique of numerous aspects of Aden's existence. She'd prefaced the speech with a claim that what she was about to say was out of her great love for him, as well as a fervent desire to see him do better. While there'd been an element of reassurance in that statement, in the end it'd done little to cushion his bruised feelings. In truth, he'd been right on the edge of weeping in that last moment before the woman in black's arrival. That was how bad he was feeling about himself in the wake of Emily's scathing assessment.

She'd criticized virtually every facet of his daily work and life habits, accusing him of laziness in the home while bemoaning a lack of the drive necessary to get ahead in his career. She didn't like how he spent so much of his downtime at home just sitting around and watching things on TV, time that, according to her, could be better spent on any number of home improvement projects. She went on to list many examples of things he could do in that area, more than a few of which would require him to buy expensive tools and learn complicated new skills he did not currently possess.

When he'd asked in a light, semi-joking tone if she believed he should have no free time whatsoever, she accused him of not being a sufficiently serious man. Men of previous generations, she told him, had not hesitated to sacrifice in every conceivable way to provide for their families. They were manly men who would sooner cut off their own hands than waste their days lounging around or playing video games.

She asked him, "Do you expect to marry me and father children with me?"

He'd not known the true answer to that—what *he* wanted—but he suspected the conversation would unfurl along an even more uncomfortable direction were he to say, "I don't know."

So he said, "Well . . . sure."

Because he did love Emily, or so he'd come to believe over the eleven months of their relationship. He was strongly enamored of her in a way that went far beyond what one experienced while in the grip of a mere crush. He wanted to be with her always and had arrived at a point where it was hard to imagine a future that didn't have her in it. There was what felt like a boundless romantic and sexual longing.

If that didn't count as love, what even *was* love?

But it turned out that "Well, sure" was as inadequate a response as "I don't know."

Emily wanted only resolute statements of intent from any man who sought to spend the rest of his life with her. Anything to the contrary she could only interpret as a red flag.

Aden opened his mouth to issue a more definitive statement regarding his intentions, but Emily pressed on, speaking rapidly as she overrode him, letting him know she'd been stewing on these things a while and felt compelled to get it all out in the open now before it overwhelmed her.

She told him about how he needed to be more aggressive and assertive at work, asserting that it was unacceptable that he hadn't earned a single promotion or raise in the nearly full year they'd been dating.

She was disappointed in general with his lack of high standards in the way he presented himself to the world. He needed to groom himself better and wear nicer clothes, make himself into the sort of man other men would look upon with respect and envy when he was out and about in the world. Using her phone, she showed him examples of items he should add to his wardrobe. A lot of it looked uncomfortable and expensive. He really wasn't sure where he was supposed to get all this extra money for fancy new clothes and a wide range of home improvement tools, but by then that was the least of his concerns.

At the end of it, she told him, "After work tonight, you will start to come up with a comprehensive plan. An actionable roadmap to a better you. You will write it out in great detail, and we'll go over it together. I'll add to it where needed, and by the end of the week, you will have taken your first steps toward making it all happen."

That was when she'd excused herself to go to the bathroom, leaving a stunned Aden feeling overwhelmed from the seeming impossibility of all she was demanding, with tears on the verge of falling.

All he wanted was a nice and simple, easy life. A life of leisure and fun that wasn't relentlessly about work and striving.

Was that really such a horrible thing?

He felt distraught and at an utter loss about how to deal with his beautiful girlfriend's litany of ultimatums.

An instant after Emily disappeared down the hallway to the bathroom, the slender woman in black appeared seemingly out of nowhere and slid into the booth. He let out a little gasp of surprise and she uttered her first words to him before he could otherwise react: "There is a better way."

She spoke with an accent he couldn't place except that it sounded vaguely European. He never learned her name, but her funereal attire prompted him to think of her simply as the woman in black. He also never got an unobstructed look at her face, hidden as it was by the black veil attached to her black hat. It was of the denser, harder-to-see-through type, affording him only a vague sense of the outline of her face. The veil, her long-sleeved black dress, and black gloves all made him think she must have just come from a graveside service, though it struck him as a bit odd that she was still wearing the veil in a diner. He wanted to ask her about it but was afraid she'd think him rude, so he asked one of the other obvious questions.

Not *who are you?*

Nor even *what are you doing in my booth?*

But, instead, "A better way to *what*?"

Despite not being able to clearly see her face, he sensed she smiled behind the veil. "Please excuse my presumptuousness, but I have good intentions, I assure you. Likewise, I hope I do not offend by saying that your woman has disrespected you in egregious, inexcusable fashion."

Aden frowned, glancing around at other nearby booths and tables, most of which were empty now with the breakfast crowd clearing out for the day. Most of his attention prior to now had been Emily, but he'd taken no note of this woman until her sudden arrival and couldn't understand how that was possible. If nothing else, he should've noticed her for the pleasing way the dress conformed to her feminine shape. It was not the sort of thing one was supposed to focus on when confronted with a woman in funeral garb, but he couldn't help himself. Her form was too enticing. Not noticing would be like looking upon a piece of classic art from one of the great masters and feeling unmoved on any level.

He hadn't seen her, though, he was sure of it.

And yet here she was now, no denying that.

Breaking off his survey of the diner's sparsely populated interior, he looked straight at her again. "You were eavesdropping?"

She nodded.

His first instinct was to tell the woman any issues he was having with Emily were none of her business. He got as far as opening his mouth to say exactly that when he hesitated, a frown again creasing his face because a part of him did feel disrespected. Until that point, his primary takeaway from Emily's speech was that he was a deeply flawed and unserious person who was lacking on too many levels. All he'd been able to think about was how bad he felt about himself as a man, but now this stranger's words were stirring something else inside him.

Was it possible Emily had treated him in an unfair and meanspirited way not out of a desire to see him improve but as a means of asserting power over him?

Had she, in fact, been a little bit of a disrespectful bitch?

"Huh."

The stranger reached across the table and clasped hands with him. Despite the glove encasing her hand, a chill rippled through his body at the moment of contact. Later, he would recognize this as his first hint of something mystical and perhaps not of the natural world about the woman. He was unnerved enough to look toward the hallway Emily had disappeared into moments earlier, experiencing intense dread at the possibility of his girlfriend returning in time to find him in the company of a strange woman, one who was holding his hand in an inappropriately familiar and intimate way.

"A man should not accept disrespect from anyone, but this is especially true in the case of one's spouse or romantic partner." She squeezed his hand, leaned farther across the table, voice dropping to a frosty whisper. "The behavior exhibited by your woman requires either correction or rejection, an end to your relationship. You should consider no other course."

Aden laughed despite the odd chill still crawling over his skin. "Well, I don't want to end things with her. That leaves correction, and while it sounds good in theory, good luck to anyone trying to tell

Emily how to behave."

The woman leaned closer still, far enough over the table for him to feel her cold breath passing through the veil to touch his face. He felt fear but also an almost painful arousal, one intense enough to make him pray he wouldn't have to stand up any time soon.

He sensed another hidden smile as she spoke again. "That is why you must kill her."

Aden could only gape in shocked amazement at first.

Then he said, "I can't kill the woman I love. Are you crazy?"

The answer to that seemed obvious.

He tried jerking his hand away, but she held fast to it, tightening her grip to an almost painful degree. The tightened hold increased his fear but also made him aware that she'd pressed something into his hand. He couldn't see it yet, but the texture suggested it was a slim piece of crumpled foil.

"This is not a suggestion, Aden. It's a decree. I have chosen to intervene on your behalf. This is something I don't often do, but *when* I do, rejection of my assistance simply isn't an option. You will do as I say."

Aden let out a shuddery breath. "I will do as you say." Even as he echoed what she'd said, he knew how insane it was. He was scared. More than that. *Terrified.* But somehow, in the midst of that terror, his cock had become even more painfully swollen. The thought of killing Emily was appalling. He was a man who'd never seriously considered committing any act of intentional malice, much less *murder.* Yet some part of him was eager to do this terrible thing. Excited, even. This witchy woman had instilled some helpless compulsion inside him. "I will do what you say," he repeated, this time with greater fervor. "But why?"

She released her grip on him and leaned back. "In your hand you have a packet of a special powder. Later today, you will mix the powder in your lady's coffee or tea. It will bring about a mostly painless demise, but it will also plant the seed of her resurrection."

He laughed in that nervous way again. "Resurrection? You're saying she'll return from the dead? Like Jesus Christ or some movie zombie?" He shook his head, smirking in disbelief. "That's absurd. Things like that don't happen in real life. What kind of game are you playing with me?"

She made a clucking sound. "Shame on you. There is no game here. How many other things you would otherwise call absurd or inexplicable have happened since I sat down with you?" She harrumphed. "You know better."

Aden made no reply this time because she was speaking nothing but undeniable truth. His fear of her was front and center again, and some part of him longed to get up and run away from this strange woman, to keep on running until he was far away from her, but he knew it wasn't possible. She was in control. He was going nowhere until she released him from the telepathic hold she had on him, a power she wielded with effortless precision.

She nodded. "Good. I see that you understand. Here is what will happen. After the poison kills her, you will take her body out into the woods behind your home, where you will dig a deep hole and bury her in it. Ten nights hence you will return to the temporary grave and remove her from the earth. After Emily resurrects, she will be whole and healthy again, but she will have changed in ways guaranteed to ensure a happier life for you both."

Aden nodded as she spoke, but he couldn't help wondering about certain things, including how this stranger knew Emily's name. He was sure it hadn't been uttered even once during breakfast, but also how could she know he lived in a house with a wooded area behind it? It implied a disturbing degree of advanced knowledge about both of them, as well as an increasing likelihood this was no chance encounter after all. An element of stalking was involved, seemingly, only the person who'd stalked them was maybe a witch instead of some garden variety obsessive weirdo.

"In the interim, you will be unbothered by anything that has happened," the woman continued as she primly laced her fingers together. "In fact, you will barely think of it at all. You will feel a sense of perfect contentment, a lightness of spirit the likes of which you've rarely experienced."

Aden pursed his lips, made a contemplative sound. "Hm, okay, but ten days is a long time for anyone to drop out of sight. What do I tell anyone who comes around looking for Emily?"

The woman grunted. "That will not happen."

"But—"

She unlaced her fingers and held up one hand in a *stop* gesture. "Enough. No more questions from you. From this point forward, you will do only as I say and act in accordance with the instructions I have given you. Know also that I have given you another gift, one which you may or may not utilize, it will be up to you. That unusual arousal you feel? When you bury your love this evening, you may also choose to deposit your seed in the freshly turned earth. Get that look off your face. There will be no need to violate her corpse. Just put your seed in the grave. If you do this, when she is reborn, she will be pregnant with your child."

Aden thought, *What the fuck?*

As before, though he didn't say the words out loud, she appeared to sense them, a sound of amusement escaping her lips for the first time. Not some guffaw, just a soft, nearly inaudible chuckle.

"Yes, Aden, a child. It is the one part I'm leaving up to you. As for Emily, when she returns, she will no longer be the harridan who berated you earlier. She will be docile and respectful of your wishes in all things. Every future choice will be yours to make. Your word will be law, as it should be."

She scooted to the edge of her side of the booth, preparing to depart.

"Wait." Aden reached out to touch her hand, but this time when his fingers grazed glove leather, instead of an unnatural chill, he felt a small electric shock. "Ouch. Damn." He shook his hand, wincing in pain. "How—"

But she was already gone.

Just vanished as if she'd winked out of existence.

He looked up and saw Emily peering down at him with a look of confused suspicion. "Who were you talking to just now?" She glanced toward the diner's entrance, brow knitting as her confusion deepened. "Do you know that woman?"

Aden shook his head. "A religious freak. She just showed up and started yammering on about saving my soul. It was weird."

"Why was she dressed like she was going to a funeral?"

Aden shrugged. "No idea."

He was assailed by a dizzying range of confused feelings. In eleven months, he'd never lied to Emily in any serious way, had never been much of a fib-teller at any point in his life, thus it was surprising and more than a little unnerving that one had come so easily to his lips.

Emily's expression sharpened to a look of deeper suspicion. "That better not have been some secret girlfriend's sneaky way of seeing you."

There was no need to feign the look of shock that came over Aden's face then. "Secret girlfriend?" He shook his head in profound astonishment, laughing as if the very idea was too absurd to grasp.

"What kind of fool would sneak around with someone else when he has you waiting at home?"

Her look of suspicion slowly yielded to a look of smirking smugness. "Yeah, I didn't think so. Just know that if you ever did try anything that stupid I'd have no choice but to make your life a living hell."

Aden smiled. "Understood."

Emily grunted. "Okay, mister. Up and at 'em. Time to go."

Aden scooted to the edge of the booth, taking care to push the foil packet still clutched in his hand deep into a hip pocket before standing up. After settling the bill at the register, they left the diner, with Emily using his car to return to the house while Aden called an Uber to take him to work.

That night after dinner—and after he'd washed the dishes—he asked Emily if she'd like a cup of tea. She said yes, and there was no big drama about how the murder unfolded. He made the tea, stirred in the powder, and took the cup out to her chair in the living room, where she started drinking the poisoned beverage without hesitation. There was some tension as he waited for her to make a face or voice a complaint about the taste. After several minutes, she appeared to become sleepy, head drooping as the cup slipped from her fingers, tumbling to the carpeted floor. She slumped down in the chair, convulsed weakly a few times, and that was the end of it.

The strangest thing about it was how little emotional distress he experienced through all of it. His heart didn't race and there'd been no attack of trembling anxiety. In the aftermath, there was no sudden rush of terrified remorse. It'd been almost perfunctory.

He was not some emotionless sociopath. He felt empathy and cared for other people, sometimes even cried during sad movies. The reason for his unusually calm demeanor seemed obvious. It was some lingering witchy effect of the woman in black on his central nervous system, a form of psychic sedation. Nothing else made any sense, because he felt certain that under any other circumstance, the act of killing a human being—*any* human being, not just the woman he loved—would turn him into a quivering wreck of a man.

Murder just wasn't in his nature.

So he'd been given a supernatural assist.

With the deed done, he waited until after midnight, when he could be reasonably certain his neighbors were all in bed for the night, and then he did as he'd been told. After turning out the backyard lights, he dragged Emily's body through the unfenced yard and into the woods, continuing until he was more than fifty feet beyond the tree line.

Then he began to dig.

And dig.

Excavating a hole big enough to accommodate a grown woman's corpse was no simple matter. If anything, it was a far more labor-intensive bit of business than he'd anticipated. This was because as a general rule physical labor was not his thing. He was a numbers guy. A data guy. There was a reason he'd only ever had desk jobs. In the ordinary course of things, the closest he got to raising a sweat was changing the filter in the coffee maker in the break room. As he dug the grave, sweating more than he had at any point in his life since high school gym class, it was not lost on him that this was one of the things about him Emily had wished to change.

Another consideration was the need to bury her deep enough to reduce the chances of some animal digging her up to snack on her remains. He didn't think there were any serious predators roaming this small section of woods, but better safe than sorry.

He kept digging until he was worn out. Until he could dig no more.

After he was done, he rolled her into the hole, dropped the shovel on the ground, and opened his pants. He did this without thinking about it, an automatic act he wasn't cognizant of until his hand was on his engorged member. This time he did experience a small flicker or horror, a brief repulsion at the obscene thing he was doing. The woman in black had suggested it, yes, but he hadn't actually believed he *would* do something so gross until he *was* doing it.

His first thought at that point was this was another way he was being compelled by the witch, but she'd assured him it would be his choice. He tested the validity of that by telling himself to stop. He stopped. He peered down into the deep, dark hole, where Emily's pale, unmoving form was illuminated by a sliver of silver moonlight. She'd come to rest on her side, with her lovely face visible in perfect profile. She looked as peaceful as a sleeping baby in a crib.

A baby . . .

His hand started moving again.

After shooting his seed into the hole, he began the arduous task of filling in the grave.

Now he'd returned and it was time to begin the job of removing

Emily from the ground. This time was a little different. He didn't feel as numb to normal human emotion. A sharp twinge of apprehensive dread made him grimace as he punched the shovel blade into the earth.

What if she didn't resurrect?

What if he pulled her out of the earth only to find she was just a decomposing corpse?

An array of similar questions ripped through his brain as he began to whimper and tremble in anticipation of being exposed as nothing more than an ordinary scumbag murderer. He told himself it wasn't possible. The woman in black wasn't a delusion, nor was the unnatural power she'd exerted over him. Self-directed anger flared inside him at the mere thought. He tried his best to shove the worries and doubts out of his head as he continued to work, but it wasn't easy.

Adrenaline flooded his system, prompting him to dig faster and faster. Sweat filled his eyes. He swiped at them with hands gritty with dirt, irritating them and forcing him to stop several times. There was water in the backpack he'd brought with him. He upended a bottle over his face to flush his eyes, growing more anxious all the while, the hard job of taking Emily out of the ground stretching out, taking longer than it should.

Far longer.

After a significantly protracted period, he began to feel he was digging deeper than he had when he'd dug the grave in the first place. He initially scoffed at the thought, but the farther down he dug without encountering her body, the more pronounced the sense of worry became. Becoming frantic, he punched the shovel blade into the earth again and again at a faster rate, slinging dirt over each shoulder in a machine-like alternating pattern, the muscles in his hands, arms, and shoulders working like pistons in overdrive, straining close to the breaking point.

When he'd dug the hole the first time, he'd worked at a fast but steady pace, building a neat pile of dirt at the side of the grave. It'd been hard, exhausting work, but he'd remained calm throughout the process. This was the opposite of that. Instead of a single large pile of earth, the grave was ringed by several smaller ones. Some of the dirt didn't make it out of the hole at all, instead going straight up into the air only to rain back down into the grave behind him, some of it cascading down his back. He hardly noticed because he was too desperately consumed with the task of reaching the grave's elusive bottom.

The time to accept the terrifying truth arrived at last. Emily was no longer in the ground. It was the only logical answer, yet he remained gripped in denial's suffocating claws a while longer, tears flowing freely down his face as he continued slamming the shovel blade into the ground with ever-increasing ferocity. Knees shaking, heart thudding with pain as he struggled to catch his breath, body on the verge of total collapse. Yet he kept going, calling on every remaining scrap of feeble strength to raise the shovel one more time.

He didn't stop until he heard Emily's voice calling out to him from above.

"Looking for me, sweetie?"

At first Aden was unsure whether he'd heard her at all, thinking perhaps his fevered imagination had produced an auditory hallucination. That it was just his traitorous brain taunting him.

Then, after swiping copious tears from his eyes with the back of a hand, he looked up and saw her looming above him. She was standing at the edge of the grave in a black dress that was not what she'd been wearing on the night he'd buried her.

Her attire was not the only thing that had changed.

The flat plane of her stomach was gone, replaced by the large swell of a pregnant belly that looked ready to burst.

Unable to believe what he was seeing, again thinking his brain must be deceiving him, he squeezed his eyes shut and held them that way for several seconds. When he opened them again, Emily was still standing above him, still looking fully nine months pregnant instead of newly expecting. The witch hadn't lied, it seemed. He'd believed in it because he'd bought into everything else she'd said, yet at no point had he expected it to be like this.

He began to weep freely again, this time in overwhelming relief. Things hadn't unfolded in exactly the way he'd expected, but that was okay. The important thing was that Emily had returned. Not only that, but she would soon be bringing their child into the world. As a bonus, she would now be easier to deal with, less demanding.

What was the word the witch had used?

Oh, yes.

Docile.

Everything looked so much brighter all of a sudden. He couldn't wait for his new family to begin their lives together.

Bending slightly at the knees, Emily extended a hand, smiling sweetly as she said, "Toss up the shovel."

He did as instructed, and she snagged the implement out of the air in a smooth, one-handed grip.

Aden then began the process of trying to climb out of the hole, which was so much deeper than it'd been before. When he'd stopped digging the first time, he'd stood in the grave at about waist level, but now the top of his head was several inches below the level of the ground. Fully cognizant of this for the first time, he experienced a sense of astonishment at how frantic and desperate he'd become prior to Emily announcing her presence. He'd pushed his body nearly to the point of total collapse. His arms shook as he grabbed handfuls of earth and tried hauling himself upward, slipping and sliding back down more than once as exhaustion continued taking its toll on him. He considered asking Emily to reach down and lend a hand but he didn't want her doing that in her delicate condition. Nothing mattered more than the well-being of his child and soon-to-be-wife.

He'd just managed to hook his elbows over the edge of the grave when he looked up and saw that Emily had reversed her grip on the shovel and was holding it over her shoulder like a baseball bat.

As on that night ten days ago, the sliver of moonlight fell across her face, and for a moment he paused, helplessly entranced by her beauty as she swung the shovel around with all the force she could muster. The underside of the shovel blade clunked hard against Aden's head. Pain exploded in his skull and he cried out in whimpering agony as he fell back into the grave.

He looked up through bleary, glassy eyes as Emily tossed in the first heavy clump of dirt, which splatted across his chest hard enough to make him gag and cough. "What's happening? Why . . . why . . . are you doing this?"

Emily threw in more clumps of dirt, working fast.

She smiled again in that sliver of moonlight.

"I gave you a test, Aden, one designed to prove your worthiness, but you failed in spectacular fashion. You killed me. Or you thought you did. The point is, you didn't even hesitate. You just did it."

A clump of dirt fell across his face. He shook it off and spat more dirt from his mouth. "The woman in black . . ."

Emily didn't just smile this time.

She laughed heartily.

"You poor, pitiful man. Can't even put two and two together. In retrospect, you were never worth my time and energy. Ah well, live and learn. *I* was the woman in black, Aden. I never even left that booth at the diner. You just thought I did."

Aden frowned as more big clumps of dirt thumped down around him. "But that doesn't—"

Another big laugh from Emily interrupted him. "What, it doesn't make sense? But of course it does. It makes *perfect* sense, because you were right about at least one thing, sweetheart. I'm a witch. I played a trick, a mental sleight of hand. I planted thoughts in your head. Hypnotized you. I told you to see me walking off toward the restroom, so that's what you thought you saw. I told you to see me as a mysterious woman in black with a Romanian accent, so you saw and heard that. None of it was real. It was just me telling you what to see, hear, and feel."

Tears flowed endlessly from Aden's eyes. He no longer doubted any of what she was telling him.

A quieter chuckle from Emily as she continued chucking dirt into the hole. "And obviously you didn't poison or kill me. That was another mental suggestion, another in a string of false memories implanted by yours truly. Oh, there was a powder, but it was only a yummy sweetener for my tea. Then you traipsed out here and dug a hole. You jerked off into it. I watched from behind a tree. It was hilarious. But you didn't put a body in the hole."

A bigger clump of dirt fell across his face. This time he swallowed some of it before he was able to spit the rest out. "But . . . the pregnancy?"

She laughed again as she paused long enough to smack the swell of her belly. "Oh, this? Just my idea of a joke. I'm not actually pregnant. It's a prosthetic, the type actors use to appear ripe with child onscreen. I'll bury it with you."

She ripped it out and tossed it down.

Aden raised a shaky, beseeching hand. "Please . . . don't do this . . . I . . . I . . . love you."

A heavy pile of dirt fell over his face yet again.

Emily nodded. "Of course you love me. I'm extraordinary. But you, sweetie, are *far* from extraordinary. You're not only weak in body and mind, you are lacking in will and inner strength. I'm honestly a bit disappointed in myself for ever thinking you might be the one for me, but life goes on." Another chuckle. "For some of us. My quest for true love will continue, and one day I'll find my real prince, I'm sure of it. I do want to thank you, though. For putting the house in my name. For transferring the contents of your bank accounts to mine before coming back out here tonight. You did provide for me to some degree, after all. That's something, right? Take a little bit of comfort in that, Aden."

The dirt continued to fall upon him.

Burying him.

Until he couldn't see.

Until he could scarcely breathe.

As more inches of dirt piled atop him, he could still faintly hear Emily for a short while longer, prettily singing "Que Sera Sera (Whatever Will Be, Will Be)."

After a little bit longer, even that faded away to nothing.

And soon, so did Aden.

JUST TO WATCH IT DIE

BOONE ATWATER HAD JUST SETTLED in for a night of watching wrestling when he heard the noise from outside, a faint rustling followed by what could have been the crunch of a stick breaking beneath the tread of someone's shoe. Kicked back in his old but comfy recliner, he paused in the act of bringing a forkful of mac and cheese to his mouth, ears straining as he waited to hear a repetition of the sound.

The blare of the television wasn't helping matters, with the wrestling announcers bleating in their usual histrionic manner about tonight's long-awaited grudge matchup. Sticking the fork back in the bowl, he set his meal aside on the foldable tray table next to the recliner, and picked up the remote, carrying it with him as he got up and went to a window at the front of the house. Once he arrived at the window, he pointed the remote at the television, muting it. He figured silencing it too soon might put a trespasser in a higher state of alert. If someone up to no good was on his property after dark, he didn't want to spook them into scurrying off before he could visually confirm it.

He stuck two fingers between slats of the blind, parting them by less than an inch, just wide enough to put his eye to the gap and look outside. No one was in the yard that he could see, unless they were way off to the side somewhere, beyond the edge of his peripheral vision, but a car with its engine running was parked directly in front of his house. Its headlights were off, but from the shape of it, he guessed it was an older style sedan, long and boxy. Boone didn't have a lot of close friends, nor did he know a lot of people in general outside of work, but he was certain he didn't know anyone who had an older ride like that. And if he did, they wouldn't drop by unannounced.

The sight of the mystery vehicle idling outside his house made his heart thud. That it was there at all at a time when he wasn't expecting visitors was unsettling enough, but the headlights being off was what bothered him the most. It'd been full dark for almost an hour, and the nearest streetlamp had burned out almost a week ago. Anyone with an innocent reason for being on this street this late would have their goddamn lights on.

Vivid scenarios sprang to life in his head, none of which he liked. The person in the car might be a garden variety bad guy staking out a house that looked like it might be vulnerable. Or a whole team of home invaders might be behind those dark windows. It was impossible to tell.

His house sat at the end of a block. The neighboring house to his right was a duplex, the closest side of which was currently unoccupied. A young-ish couple lived in the house across from him, but they were on vacation, a thing he knew only because he'd watched as they'd loaded suitcases into their SUV before driving off a few days earlier. Factor in the dead streetlamp, and it all added up to the little area outside his house having a bit of a lonely, isolated feeling. A bad guy desperate for things to pawn for drug money might think that made him and his house an easy target.

Backing away from the window, his heart pumped harder as his breathing quickened. Boone turned and stumbled his way over to the recliner, the fear rising inside him turning him clumsy. His phone was in its usual spot on the folding table next to the cooling bowl of mac and cheese. He snatched it up and walked out of the living room and down a short hallway to his bedroom. This took hardly any time at all because his house was tiny, with less square footage than a basic two-bedroom apartment.

The trembling in his hand worsened as he grabbed at the top-drawer handle on his nightstand, forcing him to make three attempts before he was able to get a firm grip on it and rip it open. He pulled at it so hard the drawer came all the way off the slider, dumping its contents on the floor.

Including his gun.

Screeching through gritted teeth in frustration, he scooped the weapon up, checked that it was loaded, and dashed back out to the living room. What he'd originally meant to do was peek through the blinds again with his thumb hovering over the button to call 911 if it looked like anyone was trying to break in. The gun was his last resort contingency. He'd only use it if he thought his life was in imminent danger. What changed things was the overload of adrenaline sizzling through his veins, turning his fear into dangerous anger. Instead of pausing to peek outside, he went right to the front door, unlocked it, hauled it open, and stepped out onto the porch, flipping the gun's safety off as he pointed it at the street.

Which was empty.

There was no sign of the idling sedan.

Boone let out a big breath and tried his best to calm, needing a few minutes before he was fully able to stop shaking. When he was again breathing evenly, he stepped down from the porch and walked out to the street. The tiny house had an appropriately small front lawn. Getting to the street took only seconds. Once there, he looked up and down the avenue, seeing cars parked here and there in driveways and at the curb, but nothing that resembled the sedan.

He stood at the edge of the street a short while longer, waiting to see if the car would come back. What finally drove him back inside was the realization that if he stayed where he was long enough, a cop might come along and give him grief for brandishing a gun in public. Hell, a mean cop in the wrong kind of mood might draw down on him, maybe even shoot him for twitching at the wrong moment. Getting shot on a night when he'd only wanted to relax in his home at the end of a long and aggravating week at work was not his idea of a good time, to say the damn least. He spent a lot of his time feeling like the universe was conspiring against him, always throwing new roadblocks and petty challenges in front of him just when he thought he might get a moment to fucking breathe. It'd be nice if he could resume his interrupted evening of vegging out in front of the television.

Just a little peace, he thought. *A little rest and a little time to enjoy myself.*

Is that so much to ask?

He thought not.

Also, while he was feeling emboldened from his dash outside, he didn't want to tempt fate by lingering out here in the open. It felt too much like daring the mystery driver to return, and a significant part of him remained fearful of how things might go in a direct confrontation with a serious aggressor.

As soon as he was back inside, he closed and locked the door, rattled the handle to be extra sure it was secure, and returned to the window to peek between blind slats again. Though only a few seconds had passed since his last glimpse of the street, he was relieved to find it still empty. Still not quite trusting the permanence of the car's disappearance, he maintained his position at the window for a good while, watching for and dreading its possible return. If it did come back, his new plan was to stay where he was and call 911 the instant it showed up. A repeat appearance in the same spot should merit a drive-by from a patrol car, right? It might not constitute absolute proof of sinister intent, but it had to count as legitimately suspicious.

His tense grip on the phone didn't begin to loosen until nearly ten minutes after he'd come back inside. A few cars passed by during that time, but none of them were the old sedan. Each vehicle had its headlights on. None of them moved at the slow, prowling speed of a predatory driver scoping out the place.

At last, he decided he could safely make a tentative attempt to return to his modest agenda for the evening, which consisted of dinner and wrestling, followed maybe by a late movie and a few beers before bed.

After engaging the safety on his gun, he set it carefully down on the folding table next to the recliner, along with his phone. The television was still on mute, and he eyed the action unfolding on the screen with a scowl as he picked up his bowl of mac and cheese, brought the fork to his mouth, and took a little bite to test the temperature. As he'd feared, it had gone completely cold.

"Goddammit. Fucking interfering motherfucker with his shitty-ass old fucking car. Why'd you have to get lost in my neck of the woods?"

Because that was the far more benign alternate theory that'd started taking shape in his head over the last couple minutes. He lived in a sprawling old urban neighborhood where the way the streets were laid out didn't always make intuitive sense. Someone trying to find their way through the area without knowing how to get around might well choose to stop briefly at the side of the road and try to get their bearings. Even with GPS, it could sometimes be confusing, as he knew from talking to more than one foreign-born Uber Eats driver. The more he thought about it, the more likely it seemed this was the true explanation behind tonight's drama. He was glad there'd been no one here to witness his overreaction. Getting labeled a paranoiac by any of his few remaining semi-close friends would be almost too embarrassing to stand.

Still muttering in annoyance, he carried the bowl into the kitchen, meaning to zap it in the microwave for a minute. Because Boone was staring at the lumpy, orange-coated noodles in the bowl, the presence of the stranger standing near the back door didn't register until he was already through the archway and several strides into the kitchen.

Then he stopped in his tracks halfway to the microwave, catching a glimpse of the man in the periphery of his vision. Even then, the reality of it didn't fully hit home until he turned his head and looked straight at him. The instant this happened, he gasped in shock, the paper bowl and its cargo of cheesy noodles slipping from his fingers to the floor. His chest lurched in a painful way as his body was again racked by uncontrollable tremors.

A multitude of powerful emotions flashed through him at the same time, the strongest being the return of his fear, which was worse than before, now that undeniable proof of a threat was standing right in front of him, no more than ten feet away. Behind that was anger over this violation of the sanctity of his home. He could see that the lock on the back door was busted. The man must have parked somewhere else and hopped the fence to come through the back way, kicking the door open while he was standing out on the street, gawping around like an idiot. Then there was a not insignificant level of bitter annoyance at having his evening interrupted yet again.

He was also more than a little confused about the man's appearance.

The intruder was wearing a rubber mask in the shape of a dog's head. A German shepherd, Boone was pretty sure. It was a well-made mask, fairly realistic looking, the kind that covered the entire head. He was also wearing a zippered black jacket, black leather gloves, and black cargo pants. Black hiking boots completed the ensemble. Even without the mask to conceal his identity, this would clearly be the garb of someone up to no good.

After an initial hoarse attempt at speech, Boone loudly cleared his throat. "Who the fuck are you?"

The stranger lifted one black-gloved hand to his neck, slipping his fingers beneath the bottom edge of the mask to touch something. A somewhat muffled and mechanically altered voice emerged from behind the mask. "*Just to watch it die.*"

Just that and nothing else before falling silent.

Boone was so flummoxed by this, all he could do was stammer and gawp for several seconds before he was finally able to push out a single semi-coherent word: "Wh-wh . . . what?"

The stranger's distorted voice again resonated beneath the thick rubber, and he remained as still as a statue as he repeated what he'd already said, this time with more vehemence and volume. "*Just to watch it die.*"

His fingers were not beneath the mask for this second utterance, perhaps because all he'd done the first time was touch the voice modulator's power button. The use of the device was puzzling. Either this was someone he knew who didn't want him to recognize his voice or it was some unknown nutcase using it simply to sound extra creepy. Mission accomplished, in either case.

After a moment of feeling like it was stuck in neutral, Boone's brain slipped back into gear, and it came to him that *he* was likely the "it" referred to in the repeated sentence. He didn't know why the man would phrase it in such a strange way, but what did that matter? The only salient fact here was that this man was here to kill him—or at least cause him serious harm—for reasons unknown. He thought about his gun out in the living room, recognizing now that his survival depended on getting to it before the obviously younger and fitter man could get to him.

The stranger pulled down the zipper of his jacket and reached a gloved hand inside, an action that at last spurred Boone into action. He turned and ran out of the kitchen, making it into the hallway and then through the archway back into the living room before the masked man caught up with him. Something hard crashed down against the crown of his skull when he was within about six feet of the recliner. The blow was delivered with enough force to drop him immediately to his knees, crippling, mind-obliterating pain exploding inside his skull. His torso flopped forward a split-second after his knees struck the hardwoods.

At first the whole of his attention was focused on the horrible pain, which was severe enough to feel life-threatening, but then he felt the wetness leaking from the wound to his head. Blood. Whatever the man had struck him with had opened a gash in his flesh. He'd heard stories of people dying from a single heavy blow of that type. The possibility was terrifying enough to prompt another attempt to get to the gun. He braced his trembling hands on the floor and tried pushing himself up.

"*Just to watch it die.*"

The altered voice came from directly above him.

A booted foot stomped down on his lower back, making him cry out in fresh pain as he was driven back to the floor. The masked man knelt next to him and roughly turned him over, heaving Boone's two-hundred-pound body around as easily as another man might toss a sack of garbage into a dumpster.

He whined at the sight of a claw hammer gripped in the man's right hand. A smear of bright red coated its silver head. Seeing his own blood made him queasy as his attacker leaned over him and raised the hammer. Another high-pitched sound of distress issued from his quivering lips as he anticipated the tool's merciless descent.

He sniffled. "Why are you doing this? What have I ever done to you?"

"*Just to watch it die.*"

The hammer came down, smashing against his top row of teeth, the hard blow shattering several right in the center. Boone screamed and gagged as blood and tooth fragments filled his mouth. He turned his head and spat out what he could, but then the hammer came down again, the hardest blow yet cracking against his jaw. Another moaning scream. The hammer went up and it came down, the blood-smeared silver head fracturing his cheekbone. Still more blows followed. His lower lip was pulped as some bottom row teeth were pulverized. Another impact mashed his nose, turning it sideways as it broke cartilage. Through it all, more sounds of pain and distress emerged from his mouth, little sprays of bloody spittle accompanying each ragged breath.

His whole life, he'd never imagined it was possible to hurt this bad. He'd been through some shit. A broken leg. A car crash that left him with a wonky back. Savage beatings at the hands of his alcoholic father as a child. But all of it put together was but the merest smidgen of the sheer, unrelenting misery consuming him now. If he had any trace of manly pride remaining, he would feel shame at how easily he'd been taken down. *Manly pride.* A total fucking joke. He'd been utterly incapable of putting up any kind of fight at all. He was incapacitated by pain, intimidated into total submission by the strength of his assailant. All he could do was whine and pitifully beg for mercy.

And he still had no idea why this was happening.

Was there even a real reason for it at all outside of psychosis?

"Wh-why . . . why . . . ?"

The relentless hammer blows had at least temporarily ceased. He could see the man's brown eyes peering at him through the eyeholes of the mask. Identifying a man from his eyes alone was next to impossible, of course, but he was sure there was nothing familiar in them. Was this really just some random sadist who'd picked him to torture and mutilate on nothing more than a whim? Because if so, it made a twisted kind of sense, the way his whole life often seemed like no more than one long unbroken string of bad luck breaks.

More whimpering and, "Why, just why . . . tell me . . . why . . ."

The man only stared at him for a long stretch of seconds, but then he backed carefully away from Boone by a few feet, keeping his grip on the hammer as he went into a hands-and-knees crouch. He stayed like that for another miserably long stretch of seconds, those brown eyes regarding him with apparent impassiveness. Just when it seemed he might remain like that forever, silent and watchful, a low sound like a deep-throated, rumbling growl became audible from behind the mask.

More pain flared as Boone lifted his head for a better look at what the psycho was doing. As soon as he did that, the assailant shifted position, lowering his torso, putting his head closer to the floor. The growling sound got louder.

He shook his head from side to side.

And he barked. Like a dog. The sound as eerily distorted as that single intelligible utterance he kept repeating.

Urine stained Boone's trousers as he made a sound like a cross between a strained laugh and another terrified whimper.

What. The. Fuck?

He spat out more blood and coughed.

"Are you insane?"

The man grabbed hold of Boone's right wrist and held his hand pinned to the floor, forcing him to splay his fingers flat. With his other hand, the man raised the hammer again. Before Boone could think to clench his fingers into a fist, the man's blunt instrument of bodily destruction descended numerous times in rapid succession, the head crushing and breaking slender finger bones, popping fingernails into many brittle pieces. Boone screeched and tried with all his might to tear his hand free, but the man's grip was too strong, impossible to budge. The hammer smashed and smashed, reducing his fingers to useless, bloody lengths of floppy, flat flesh. Boone turned his head and looked up at the folding table next to the recliner, thinking of the gun he couldn't see from the floor. If he could get to it now by some miracle, would he even be able to use it? And if he could, who would he use it on, the assailant or himself to stop the horrible fucking agony?

He didn't know.

All he could do was weakly say *Why?* over and over.

"*Just to watch it die. Just to watch it die. JUST TO WATCH IT DIE!*"

Punctuated with more distorted growling, barking and head shaking.

As time stretched out, Boone considered the question of who in the world could hate him enough to do this. While it was true he didn't have many close friends, he also didn't have any real enemies, not since maybe high school a third of a century ago, and he couldn't imagine who could harbor some stupid adolescent grudge for that long. Not to mention that this guy couldn't possibly be old enough to be one of his former classmates.

This just about had to be some random crazy person who'd fixated on him for no remotely sane reason. Some unmedicated mental patient he'd looked at the wrong way at the grocery store one time. Something like that. Nothing else made any goddamn sense.

He lifted his head again after belatedly realizing the hammer blows had once again ceased. The assailant was no longer in his weird crouch and was instead back to kneeling at Boone's side. He was breathing more heavily after all the exertion with the hammer, making the inside of the mask vibrate audibly. The eyes stared at him through the holes, still conveying a strange calmness belying everything else about the man's behavior.

Boone's throat rattled as he did his best to clear it of blood and mucus. "I don't deserve this . . . this cruelty. How could you do this to me? How?"

His voice was plaintive and strained, crackling with hoarseness.

The man stared silently at him another few seconds.

Then he reached up and pulled the mask off his head, tossing it aside.

Boone frowned when he saw the man's unfamiliar face. "Who are you?"

The man's expression was flat, unreadable, betraying no emotion despite the frenzy of brutal violence. His cheeks were red and his forehead was sheened with sweat, but otherwise he appeared completely unaffected by what he'd done. He was young-ish, somewhere in his early thirties. His brown hair was short and bristly, and his face was surprisingly roundish for a man so fit. He was neither handsome nor ugly, just sort of ordinary. Bland. Boone dredged his memory, straining to recall if he'd ever seen this person anywhere, even just in passing while out for a walk or whatever. He came up with nothing at first, but the longer he stared at the guy, the more he felt the faintest little flicker of . . . something. But that could be a false impression, his brain straining too hard to recall a memory that wasn't actually there.

He felt that flicker again. Still so faint.

"Who are you?"

The man's flat expression changed for the first time, a little twitch of a smile as he removed the strapped-on voice modulator the mask had hidden, tossing it aside as well. "I killed a dog one time. Crazy shit, boys. Crazy shit."

His voice sounded strange. Not distorted. But not right, either. It was a voice that didn't match the face. It was a put-on, an exaggerated mockery of a stereotypical southern redneck voice.

Boone sputtered in confusion. "Wh-what?"

The man's voice changed again. Became less redneck. Incredulous. "What you saying, Booner? You mean you hit a dog with your car? Ran over a pooch?"

More noises of confusion from Boone even as that faint flicker in his head abruptly got a bit livelier. There was something there. Something distant, far beneath the surface, an echo from somewhere way back in time.

The stranger's voice shifted back to redneck parody. "Nah, man, it weren't no accident. I shot the thing. Just to watch it die." Snickering, he poked an index finger against the side of his head. "Put the muzzle right here and squeezed the goldang trigger." Now he made a gesture with his hand to mime blood pumping out the other side of his head. "Y'all should've seen it. Blood spurting like a little red firehose. Then the mutt just fell over. It was a trip and a half."

The incredulous other voice returned, accompanied by a look of sneering disgust. "Oh, man, that's fucked up, Boone. Why'd you even tell us that?"

Then he fell silent, expression flat again as he stared down at the face of the man he'd already fucked up beyond recognition.

Boone stared at the stranger's face and wept.

It'd come back to him now, the flicker intensifying steadily as the man had talked, dispersing the foggy veil of time, taking him back to that moment, the one that had lived on in this person's mind all this time, for over a decade. He remembered him now, but he'd been leaner then, face not quite as round. In his early twenties, maybe even late teens. It'd been during that short time when he'd worked third shift in a warehouse. On break talking shit with some of the guys. The usual crap, maybe half of anything anyone said even a little bit true. Macho braggadocio. Nothing anyone could take seriously. This kid—he'd been a kid back then, anyway—was a temp. He'd only been there a few nights before disappearing forever, the way so many temps did, moving on to something better, more permanent. Even now, with the memory resurfaced, his name eluded him.

Tears flowed endlessly from Boone's eyes. "Man, I didn't even do it. I couldn't. Kill a dog like that. Don't you know that?"

His one-time coworker said nothing, just stared coldly.

Boone coughed. "I swear, man. On my mother's fucking grave. That story I told, it really happened, but it wasn't me, man. I swear to fucking God. That was something my daddy did when I was a kid. It haunted me. I mean it. I couldn't do something like that. I know it sounds fucked up, but I passed it off that night as something I did just to make myself sound tough, like someone not to be fucked with. Like a mean and ornery son of a bitch. The kind of man my father was. It was dumb, I know, but you can't kill me over it."

The man looked away for a moment, a look of contemplation on his face. A faint, fluttering hope dawned inside Boone. Was it possible he'd reached the guy with his desperate, impassioned speech? He wanted to believe it was possible. As horrible as the pain was, there were such things as morphine and surgery. His smashed-up hand was probably a lost cause, but all his injuries so far would be survivable with the right care. Another thing bolstering that little tickle of hope was knowing this guy had held onto this level of rage for this length of time over an animal. An animal he'd never met or known. More like the *idea* of an animal, really. Yes, he was capable of extreme violence, but even that was motivated by compassion and empathy, by a deep and enduring desire to avenge an innocent and trusting creature that hadn't been able to protect itself. Because if he wasn't going to do it, who would? That was how Boone imagined the guy thought of it, anyway.

Theoretical capacity for empathy aside, he still thought the guy was a goddamn lunatic. He could understand someone being upset over the story he'd told. Looking back, it'd definitely been a dumb thing to share, but he'd always been tired and kind of loopy on third shift, coasting on amphetamines, his judgment not what it should be. Still, for someone—anyone—to hold on to that anger at a stranger for so many years, keeping track of where he moved, biding time with ungodly patience, waiting until long, long after anyone would ever think to connect the two of them . . . well, if that wasn't crazy, what was?

The man looked at him, his expression cold again. "Here's the thing, Boone, I don't know if I believe you. The truth is, at this point, it doesn't even matter. Maybe your daddy did it while you watched, and maybe you told the truth the first time all those years ago. Either way, it happened, and you're connected to it. And maybe worst of all you thought it was an okay thing to say to a kid who had his own beloved pet killed by a redneck asshole once upon a time."

Real anger surged inside Boone. He rocked himself over onto his side, then into a half-sitting position on his elbow. "How was I supposed to know that, you cocksucking piece of shit!? Am I fucking psychic? Fuck you." He hocked up a wad of bloody phlegm and spat it at the intruder, splashing the tops of his hiking boots. "And goddammit, it was just an animal. You can't kill a man over something like that, even if he did it."

The stranger appeared to think about it again.

Then he nodded, smiling.

"But that's where you're wrong, Boone. Dead wrong."

He moved fast, too fast for Boone to react, retrieving the rubber dog mask. The next thing Boone knew, it was being pulled down over his own head, and for a moment he couldn't breathe with the rubber tight against his sweaty flesh, but the man kept pulling the mask down, tugging at it until the molded interior aligned better with the shape of his features and knocking him back to the ground.

Then he climbed off him, moving out of sight for barely more than a second. When the man reappeared above him, it was with

Boone's gun in his hand, aimed at its owner's masked face.

Boone moaned in hopeless, abject misery. "No. You can't."

The man shook his head. "I can, though. Just to watch you die."

Boone watched the gloved finger squeeze the trigger.

He opened his mouth, hoping he'd have just enough time to say one last thing, to throw his defiant final confession in this mangy, mutt-loving motherfucker's face, but it was too late.

"I—"

The bullet punched through the center of his forehead.

The stranger stood there a while, watching with satisfaction as blood leaked out of the mask.

Somewhere, on some ethereal level of existence, an old canine soul was resting easier, he was sure of it. He removed the bloody mask from the dead man's head, feeling the weight of an old burden lift from his shoulders as he walked out through the back and disappeared into the night.

Two-time Splatterpunk Award winner Bryan Smith is the author of numerous novels and novellas, including *Depraved*, *68 Kill*, *Slowly We Rot*, *The Killing Kind*, and *The Freakshow*. He is also the co-author of *Suburban Gothic*, written with Brian Keene. A new novel entitled *Monstrous* is forthcoming from Flame Tree Press in 2026. An acclaimed film version of *68 Kill* was released in 2017. His story "Every Dog Has Its Day" was included in the New York Times bestselling anthology *The End of the World As We Know It: Tales of Stephen King's The Stand*. He lives in the Midwest with his dog Mac and has an enduring affinity for strong, bitter beer and loud rock music of an increasingly ancient vintage.

Social media:
bryansmith.bsky.social

Journal and exclusive fiction:
patreon.com/TheHorrorofBryanSmith

One Night at the Skull Spark Club playlist
(aka DNA of the Bile Lords):
https://open.spotify.com/playlist/4m1CmmalL-wfQyKxcIZJt1n?si=d98beb438889463a

Other Grindhouse Press Titles

#666__*Satanic Summer* by Andersen Prunty
#114__*Thrill Killers* by Steven Caumo
#113__*The Landlord* by C.V. Hunt and Andersen Prunty
#112__*The Freakshow: Rebirth in Drayton Falls, Volume 2* by Bryan Smith
#111__*Drive-Thru of the Dead: Drayton Falls, Volume 1* by Bryan Smith
#110__*Inhospitable* by Ali Seay
#109__*Violência* by Sultan Z. White
#108__*From the Void* by Bryan Smith
#107__*Corpse Mountain* by Andersen Prunty
#106__*Depraved Halloween* by Bryan Smith
#105__*Dread Ink* by Bryan Smith
#104__*Jack and Mr. Grin* by Andersen Prunty
#103__*What Ever Happened to Jo Rose?* by Chris DiLeo
#102__*I Think I'm Alone Now* by Ali Seay
#101__*Cute Aggression* by Emily Lynn
#100__*Headless* by Scott Cole
#099__*The Killing Kind* by Bryan Smith
#098__*An Affinity for Formaldehyde* by Chloe Spencer
#097__*Kill The Hunter* by Bryan Smith
#096__*The Gauntlet* by Bryan Smith
#095__*Bad Movie Night* by Patrick Lacey
#094__*Hysteria: Lolly & Lady Vanity* by Ali Seay
#093__*The Prettiest Girl in the Grave* by Kristopher Triana
#092__*Dead End House* by Bryan Smith
#091__*Graffiti Tombs* by Matt Serafini
#090__*The Hands of Onan* by Chris DiLeo
#089__*Burning Down the Night* by Bryan Smith
#088__*Kill Hill Carnage* by Tim Meyer
#087__*Meat Photo* by C.V. Hunt and Andersen Prunty
#086__*Dreaditation* by Andersen Prunty
#085__*The Unseen II* by Bryan Smith
#084__*Waif* by Samantha Kolesnik
#083__*Racing with the Devil* by Bryan Smith
#082__*Bodies Wrapped in Plastic and Other Items of Interest* by Andersen Prunty
#081__*The Next Time You See Me I'll Probably Be Dead* by C.V. Hunt
#080__*The Unseen* by Bryan Smith
#079__*The Late Night Horror Show* by Bryan Smith

#078__*Birth of a Monster* by A.S. Coomer
#077__*Invitation to Death* by Bryan Smith
#076__*Paradise Club* by Tim Meyer
#075__*Mage of the Hellmouth* by John Wayne Comunale
#074__*The Rotting Within* by Matt Kurtz
#073__*Go Down Hard* by Ali Seay
#072__*Girl of Prey* by Pete Risley
#071__*Gone to See the River Man* by Kristopher Triana
#070__*Horrorama* edited by C.V. Hunt
#069__*Depraved 4* by Bryan Smith
#068__*Worst Laid Plans: An Anthology of Vacation Horror* edited by Samantha Kolesnik
#067__*Deathripping: Collected Horror Stories* by Andersen Prunty
#066__*Depraved* by Bryan Smith
#065__*Crazytimes* by Scott Cole
#064__*Blood Relations* by Kristopher Triana
#063__*The Perfectly Fine House* by Stephen Kozeniewski and Wile E. Young
#062__*Savage Mountain* by John Quick
#061__*Cocksucker* by Lucas Milliron
#060__*Luciferin* by J. Peter W.
#059__*The Fucking Zombie Apocalypse* by Bryan Smith
#058__*True Crime* by Samantha Kolesnik
#057__*The Cycle* by John Wayne Comunale
#056__*A Voice So Soft* by Patrick Lacey
#055__*Merciless* by Bryan Smith
#054__*The Long Shadows of October* by Kristopher Triana
#053__*House of Blood* by Bryan Smith
#052__*The Freakshow* by Bryan Smith
#051__*Dirty Rotten Hippies and Other Stories* by Bryan Smith
#050__*Rites of Extinction* by Matt Serafini
#049__*Saint Sadist* by Lucas Mangum
#048__*Neon Dies At Dawn* by Andersen Prunty
#047__*Halloween Fiend* by C.V. Hunt
#046__*Limbs: A Love Story* by Tim Meyer
#045__*As Seen On T.V.* by John Wayne Comunale
#044__*Where Stars Won't Shine* by Patrick Lacey
#043__*Kinfolk* by Matt Kurtz
#042__*Kill For Satan!* by Bryan Smith
#041__*Dead Stripper Storage* by Bryan Smith

#040__*Triple Axe* by Scott Cole
#039__*Scummer* by John Wayne Comunale
#038__*Cockblock* by C.V. Hunt
#037__*Irrationalia* by Andersen Prunty
#036__*Full Brutal* by Kristopher Triana
#666__*Satanic Summer* by Andersen Prunty
#035__*Office Mutant* by Pete Risley
#034__*Death Pacts and Left-Hand Paths* by John Wayne Comunale
#033__*Home Is Where the Horror Is* by C.V. Hunt
#032__*This Town Needs A Monster* by Andersen Prunty
#031__*The Fetishists* by A.S. Coomer
#030__*Ritualistic Human Sacrifice* by C.V. Hunt
#029__*The Atrocity Vendor* by Nick Cato
#028__*Burn Down the House and Everyone In It* by Zachary T. Owen
#027__*Misery and Death and Everything Depressing* by C.V. Hunt
#026__*Naked Friends* by Justin Grimbol
#025__*Ghost Chant* by Gina Ranalli
#024__*Hearers of the Constant Hum* by William Pauley III
#023__*Hell's Waiting Room* by C.V. Hunt
#022__*Creep House: Horror Stories* by Andersen Prunty
#021__*Other People's Shit* by C.V. Hunt
#020__*The Party Lords* by Justin Grimbol
#019__*Sociopaths In Love* by Andersen Prunty
#018__*The Last Porno Theater* by Nick Cato
#017__*Zombieville* by C.V. Hunt
#016__*Samurai Vs. Robo-Dick* by Steve Lowe
#015__*The Warm Glow of Happy Homes* by Andersen Prunty
#014__*How To Kill Yourself* by C.V. Hunt
#013__*Bury the Children in the Yard: Horror Stories* by Andersen Prunty
#012__*Return to Devil Town (Vampires in Devil Town Book Three)* by Wayne Hixon
#011__*Pray You Die Alone: Horror Stories* by Andersen Prunty
#010__*King of the Perverts* by Steve Lowe
#009__*Sunruined: Horror Stories* by Andersen Prunty
#008__*Bright Black Moon (Vampires in Devil Town Book Two)* by Wayne Hixon
#007__*Hi I'm a Social Disease: Horror Stories* by Andersen Prunty
#006__*A Life On Fire* by Chris Bowsman
#005__*The Sorrow King* by Andersen Prunty
#004__*The Brothers Crunk* by William Pauley III

#003__*The Horribles* by Nathaniel Lambert
#002__*Vampires in Devil Town* by Wayne Hixon
#001__*House of Fallen Trees* by Gina Ranalli
#000__*Morning is Dead* by Andersen Prunty

www.ingramcontent.com/pod-product-compliance
Lightning Source LLC
LaVergne TN
LVHW030922080826
845145LV00013B/3008

* 9 7 8 1 9 5 7 5 0 4 2 8 5 *